REMEMBERING US

ONE

M y steps are slow and my feet are uncertain.

The edges of the stairway I'm being pulled down are gray and cloudy from the smoke wafting up from the basement dance floor.

Kelsey is pulling me somewhere I don't want to follow.

Why don't I want to be here?

The answer niggles at the edges of my mind, but I can't pull it to the front. It's just out of my grasp, like always.

A sweaty shoulder bumps me into the wall and my hand is pulled from Kelsey's. Cold, foamy beer splashes out of a red plastic cup and hits my shoulder. Kelsey doesn't look back to see where I am, and the blond guy who hit me doesn't stop to ask if I'm okay.

I steady my feet and take another step down. The dance floor is packed with people, and the music is so loud that the thumping bass rattles my teeth. My eyes scan the dark room—brightened only by the strobe light hanging in the center of the ceiling—looking for someone.

The lump in my throat disappears when I realize he isn't here.

He's not here.

A mixture of relief and disappointment swirls inside of me. I smile and reach Kelsey at the bar. The guy next to her fills two plastic cups, but I wave mine away. His name is Zander and he's in my statistics class and is friends with Adam. I laugh at something he says as he and

Kelsey leave for the dance floor. The nervousness returns when I'm by myself, and my eyes scan the room. I should leave now, before he comes.

But then I see him, and I can't help but smile. He's a head taller than everyone else, and as he hits the bottom stair, he has to duck his head to make it through the doorway. A small section of his black hair falls into his eyes and he flips it back. As if he knows I'm here, his eyes find me immediately and he smiles, walking toward me.

His smile lights up the room and I am no longer worried. Kelsey is gone, Zander is a distant memory, and I don't know if there's music still playing.

When Adam is around me, my brain flees and my heart flip-flops. His kisses make me lose my mind and remind me of dark chocolate, full of all those feel-good hormones.

He's a few feet from me when he reaches his arm out like he wants to hug me. I take a step forward, but before my foot hits the ground, I'm bumped to the side. I blink and a tiny blonde is wrapped around Adam. Her legs are around his waist and her arms are around his shoulders. She's completely latched onto him. He smiles at me. His eyes stay on mine as he kisses her forehead and sets her to her feet.

"Hi, Amy." The little blonde scowls at me. Adam's eyes are laughing at me.

This. This is why I didn't want to be here.

∼

"So who was the girl?"

I stare at the ceiling, ignoring my therapist's question. I hate this room. The walls are yellow but not a happy yellow. More like what I imagine baby poop looks like. And the chairs haven't been updated since at least the sixties. By the time my sessions are done, the only thing that's changed is the imprint of the scratchy fabric on the backs of my thighs.

Instead of answering the question, I count the ceiling tiles and multiply the rows. Ironic that I use math at a time like this when it was a math class that got me into all this trouble in the first place.

Reliving all these dreams every week is almost as exhausting as having them in the first place. Talking about them doesn't make anything better.

"Adam?" Dr. Jamison has lost interest in my silence, again, and turns to him. She's about fifty years old and her faded blond hair that hangs down to her waist is always braided. She wears flowy, multi-colored hippy skirts and mismatched tops every time I see her. Sometimes I want to ask her if she has a joint, just to see what she says.

"Tina," Adam says softly. I stare out the window at the playground that sits empty at the park across the street. "It was just Tina."

"Who's Tina?"

"She was a friend from home. We grew up next door to each other. She was in town that weekend visiting friends from our high school that went to college with me. That's all."

That's all. It's only two words, but they sound so condescending every time I hear them. It tells me that everything I'm either dreaming or remembering is made up or a half-truth of what the real-life events actually were. It tells me that I'm being an idiot for believing them over my boyfriend who loves me. Or so I've been told.

Maybe I'd believe them if I remembered Adam at all.

"Amy, does hearing this make you feel better?"

I shrug and cross my arms over my stomach, flinching as my muscles tighten along the gash on my right side that is slowly healing. Nothing makes me feel better anymore because I can't remember anything that's happened in the last two years. I have no idea if he's lying or being honest. "It's fine."

"Fine?" Adam's voice carries a hint of anger. He flexes his fingers wide open and rubs them down the tops of his thighs. He drops his head, shakes it once, then two times, and releases a loud breath.

Kelsey keeps telling me that he's so great and kind and patient and funny and smart and blah, blah, blah. I've been hearing it for weeks now and I'm so tired of it. All I see when I look at him is frustration and anger mixed with a little bit of pain.

"Are we done? I want to go home." We have at least twenty minutes left in our session, but they're *not* helping.

I've been told for the last several weeks that my memory could return at any moment. Before I left the hospital, my neurologist, Dr. Hassen, told me that my memories could return gradually over time.

Or, everything I've forgotten about the last two years could come rushing into my brain like an avalanche within a split second. When he said that, the only thing I could think was that I hoped I wasn't driving at the time. Doesn't really seem like a safe place to be when an avalanche hits my brain, and I think I've fulfilled my accident quota for my lifetime.

I think it'd be better if it happened while I was awake. Instead, they come to me at night as dreams and I have no idea what's true and what isn't until I have to sit here and talk about them with my new therapist, dissecting them over and over again.

How do I know if they're true?

And how do I know if I'm supposed to trust the guy explaining everything to me? He may dress nice and we might live together, but every time I close my eyes I see a different version of him than the one everyone else sees during the day.

And what in the hell am I supposed to do with that?

"One more thing before you leave today, Amy." Dr. Jamison is smiling. She always smiles, regardless of what is said. She *has* to get stoned. "I have an assignment for you this week."

I raise an eyebrow and cradle my casted, broken arm with my free hand.

"I want you to ask Adam one question this week about something you guys did for the first time."

Adam tilts his head to the side. "The first time?" His cheeks are pink, and I think he might be embarrassed.

Of course he would think about sex. That seems to be the only thing the guy in my dreams *does* think about.

Dr. Jamison just smiles.

I frown.

"Any first time. First date. First phone call. Whatever. Just ask him to describe something you think you'd want to know about."

"Okay." I shrug and shift my weight to my good foot. I got a walking cast put on my left foot earlier this week and it's easier to move around now, but still uncomfortable by the end of the day.

"And I want you to believe his answer."

I make a face. How am I supposed to believe someone I don't know? Believing and trusting doesn't happen just because you say so; it happens over the course of a relationship. And from what I've dreamed, if we did have a relationship, it was at best dysfunctional.

"Fine." I turn to leave and Adam meets me at the office door, holding it open for me as I hobble through. His hand touches my lower back as I pass by, and I flinch out of his way. He lets go as soon as I do but sighs again. If I were to turn around and look at him, he'd be shaking his head. I know this because I've seen him do it a lot in the last three weeks.

I walk straight outside, leaving him to schedule our Thursday appointment. The air outside is fresh. It smells like summer is about to hit, and it makes me smile, thinking of all the hours that I've spent in the woods, hiking on trails, rock climbing, and whitewater rafting through the mountains just outside Denver. I've lived my entire life in a suburb of Denver and I've always thought it was the best place in the whole world to live.

A dull pain vibrates through my arm and I close my eyes. I rest my head against the side of Adam's black Highlander and remind myself that I won't be doing any of those things this summer. At least not until the casts come off and my wounds heal.

My booted cast scrapes across the pavement. My ankle hurts and my arm is itchy from my cast. The eight staples in the back of my head were removed last week. In their place, I have a small, square patch of hair that is just beginning to grow back. Fortunately, when the rest of my hair is down, it's easy to keep it hidden. I have a gash on my right side that runs from my hip bone almost to my breast. It looks like someone tried to slash me open with a jagged-edged knife. The skin is healing, the stitches are innumerable, and every time I turn my torso it feels like someone is trying to rip my kidney out with their bare hands.

There was a hiking accident. That's all I know. The rest is being left up to my memory, which my doctors have assured me will return. How in the hell do they know? What if I never remember?

It's been weeks since I woke up from my coma, and I don't remember anything more than the fact that I live with a stranger and I don't like him when I dream.

I'm still resting against the side of Adam's SUV, fingering the back of my scalp, when he comes outside. He stands next to me, crossing his feet at the ankles. We don't touch. That small whisper of a touch he gave me in the doorway is the first time his hands have touched me since the day I tripped in our kitchen. His arms reached out and caught me. I froze, paralyzed by having his hands on me.

He shook his head, sighed, grabbed his keys, left the apartment, and didn't come back for two hours. When he did, the scent of beer laced his breath.

"I'm sorry I keep getting frustrated with you, Ames." His head falls against the side of his SUV and he runs a hand down the front of his face. "I just miss you."

His voice trembles a little bit and he sounds sad. He looks sad. I wonder what it would feel like to see him smile again like he did the night in my dream. Until the blonde girl, Tina, jumped into his arms, he seemed happy to see me. Was he? Was I a game? If so, why am I still here? I press my fingers to my temples, hoping to stave off the beginning thumps of another headache.

"Who's Tina?"

"She was a friend, I swear." He turns to me and leans his hip against his car. "She dated my best friend, Mike, in high school and she was excited to see me. It was an innocent thing."

"So that was real?"

Not everything I dream about is real. One night, I dreamed my parents gave me a horse for my seventh birthday. I know for a fact that didn't happen. Not because we didn't have the money for one, but because there's no way my parents would have given me something I so desperately wanted. They gave me what they thought I should have. Mother knows best and all that.

He nods. "We had our second date the night before and I remember being excited to see you because you had told me you weren't coming. After I let Tina go, you threw a beer in my face."

I laugh. It sounds like something I would do. It wouldn't have been the first beer I've thrown in an asshole's face at a frat party. He laughs and I finally see something similar to the smile he gave me in my dream.

He really is handsome and I can see why I would find him attractive. He's tall and my head barely reaches his shoulders. His black hair is shaggy, but I don't know if it's always this long or if it needs a trim. His body is lean but toned, and I know from the pictures in the apartment we share that he used to play a lot of soccer.

He's handsome. A soccer player. He has a nice laugh. These are the only things I know about him.

His kisses remind me of dark chocolate, full of all those feel-good hormones.

My stomach flip-flops and I stop laughing, sobered by the memory.

"I want to go home. My parents' home," I clarify, when I remember that I live with him now and not in the apartment my best friend, Kelsey, and I shared our sophomore year of college.

My therapy sessions leave me on edge, and hearing his answers inside and outside of them doesn't help me. Everything is different and I wonder if things will ever be simple.

He sighs and his head drops. I see that happen a lot. It makes me wonder if Adam has always been this frustrated with me or if it's a new thing.

"Amy," he starts, with a defeated tone in his voice, but then stops and shakes his head. "Fine."

He opens the door to my side and then closes it harder than necessary once I've sat down. I watch his mouth move, speaking curse words I can't hear, as he walks around the front of the car, roughly running his hand through his jet-black hair. Again.

TWO

"These things will just take time." My mom, Carol, pats the top of my head like I'm her lap dog and takes her seat at the dinner table. My parents don't always like me being here and say they think it's better for me if I spend as much time as possible with Adam. But sometimes after a therapy session I need to get away from him, and the apartment that we share feels more like a cage than a home.

You would think my parents would want their daughter, who apparently almost died from a hiking accident, around all the time. But not mine. This is only my third time visiting them since I got out of the hospital, and every time I'm around them our conversations are uncomfortable—more strained than I remember.

I want to ask them what happened to make them treat me more distantly than normal. I have so many questions to ask my parents, but I know better. I will not get answers from them. The Thompsons do not discuss uncomfortable topics. Never have, never will.

My dad, Don, frowns at my mom and shakes his head, silently telling her to drop it. He used to be a partner at a corporate law firm before he ran for Senate when I was thirteen. He's been in office ever since. I know he loves me, but his ability to show any type of affection for his youngest of two daughters is about as dry as the stack of tax codes that he used to memorize for fun.

Some people spend their lives trying to keep up with the Joneses. From my parents' perspective, they *are* the Joneses and have always reveled in the fact that people try to keep up with them. To my parents—my mom in particular—image is everything.

I frown, thinking about this while I ladle some sort of strange-looking grain soup into my bowl. Quinoa something or other. It looks like white eyelashes, but it's supposed to be healthful.

Why do my parents like Adam, then? Is he rich? When I was sixteen, I wasn't allowed to go out on a date with Jackson Latner. He was the quarterback on our high school's state-championship-winning football team and a straight-A student. He was a gentleman and polite and one of the few guys at my school that treated girls with respect. His downfall? He was also a scholarship student at our private school and his parents lived in a fifteen-year-old three-bedroom duplex. He simply wasn't rich enough for me to date. He didn't come from the kind of pedigree my mom wanted for me.

Pedigree. She actually used the word, as if Jackson and I were show dogs in heat.

"Mom, why do you like Adam?" I finally ask, taking a risk and interrupting their conversation about someone who embarrassed themselves at the country club where my mom spends her morning sipping mimosas and gossiping about all the "lesser" members.

She licks her lips and takes a sip of her wine. "What's not to like about Adam?"

I turn to my dad. He's not as pretentious as my mom, but his standards for his daughters are high. "He loves you." His eyebrows turn in and he frowns, almost as if he doesn't understand my question. "Isn't that enough?"

For most people, yes. For my parents, it doesn't fit. Does Adam have money I don't know about? We live in a small, older two-bedroom apartment. Our furniture looks like the kind you would expect two twenty-two-year-olds and recent college graduates to own. It's mismatched and worn down. Our tables have water rings from glasses that didn't sit on a coaster. There is nothing about the apartment I live in with Adam that should have my parents' approval.

"And he's nice to me? You like him, really?"

My dad's knife scratches across his plate, sending his half-buttered roll skittering to the floor. My mom's eyelids flicker in rapid succession a half-dozen times before she glances to my dad and then back to her wine.

"Of course, honey." This time, there's a slight tightening around her eyes that tells me she's lying.

With a fluidity that comes from decades of avoiding uncomfortable conversations, my mother begins talking about my sister, Ann, and her happily married life. She's been married for five years and is seven years older than me. We have nothing in common and never have. But she seems to be happily married to an air force pilot. She stays home with her three-year-old son, Cooper, and my newborn niece, Tilly, whom I have yet to meet because my sister hasn't bothered to visit or call me. While I was always uncomfortable with my parents' display of their wealth and preferred to live more "normally," my sister has always thrived on the money and glamour and attention it brings. I'm a wallflower where my parents are concerned, and my sister is the beautiful social butterfly.

I don't bother asking any more questions for the rest of dinner, knowing the answers they gave me were the only ones I'd hear.

~

I hate getting dressed in the mornings. Not like I have a lot of options right now with my booted foot and casted arm, but every morning I stare at my clothes wondering, who in the hell am I?

Nothing makes sense. My Jimmy Choo shoes and UGG boots

have been replaced with sparkling red Doc Martens boots and flip-flops. My designer dresses are gone and now I'm left staring at stacks of denim and basic T-shirts. Though I rejected the elite life-style of my parents, I've always worn dresses and leggings—even in the middle of the harsh Denver winters.

My stomach churns as I stare at the boots like they're going to jump out and bite me. I'm not a Doc Martens shit-kicking boot kind of girl. This isn't me. None of it is . . . except it is. I feel tears bubbling in my eyes all over again. I bite them back, hating that after three weeks, it's a pair of shiny red rocker-type boots that finally have my walls crumbling.

And I hate the damn tears. I don't want to be weak. I never cry. At least I don't remember being such a crybaby. But every day that I'm stuck in this apartment with nothing but black holes for memo-ries, the questions assault me.

Why is all our furniture mismatched?

Why do our dressers look like they came from a garage sale?

Who am I?

What happened to me?

How did I get here?

I hate that I don't know my best friend's boyfriend, Zander. I've met him once or twice now, but apparently Kelsey is dating and also living with one of Adam's best friends from college, Zander. I was told they started dating shortly after Adam and I did. When Adam and I moved in together, Kelsey moved in with Zander.

I can feel my blood rushing through me, adrenaline and fear and confusion all mixed together. I fall to the floor, swallowing deep breaths until the tears stay away and I'm brave enough to call the one person who will answer me. The only one I can trust.

I smile when her grouchy voice answers the phone.

"It's eight in the morning, Amy. What in the hell do you need this early?"

"Sorry." Kelsey is worthless before nine in the morning and a twenty-ounce mug of coffee. Minimum. "I just need some help. Can you come over in a little bit?"

She groans and I imagine her rolling over in bed, stretching. "Fine. I'll swing by Hash and be there in thirty minutes. But you're paying for it when I get there."

I groan my approval. Their bagels are to die for. Crunchy on the outside, soft and chewy on the inside, and always melt-in-your-mouth warm. I've had an addiction to them since I was ten. "I'm going to take a bath, so if I don't answer the door, just let yourself in."

Her grouchiness changes to concern. "Do you need any help?"

I shake my head even though she can't see me. "No, I've been able to figure it out lately."

We say our good-byes and I hobble my broken and casted body toward the bathroom. For the first two weeks after I got out of the hospital, Kelsey came over every day to help me wash my hair and get cleaned up. It's embarrassing to be twenty-two years old and not able to take care of yourself. There was no way my mother would have wanted to help, and I didn't want Adam's help. Considering he's a guy, and close to a stranger, there was no way I was letting him bathe me. Kelsey was my last option but my first choice. We grew up together, tried on our first training bras together, and lucky for me, she's a nurse now, so she's totally comfortable with it.

Once my casted arm is bagged, my stitches are covered, and my booted leg is draped over the edge of the tub, I do the best I can with the movable showerhead, trying to clean myself in just a couple of inches of bathwater.

A rustling in the bedroom through the open bathroom door startles me, but I calm down when I realize Kelsey has probably gotten here with breakfast.

"Hey, Kels! Can you come help me?" I shout through the slightly opened door.

I'm just about to yell for her again when the door creaks open. I stop shaving my leg, look up . . . and freeze.

"Get out!" I yell, when I realize Adam is staring at me from the doorway, and I'm completely naked. It sends a tingly feeling down my spine. "Adam! Out!"

I look around for a towel, but I must have forgotten to get one out of the cupboard because there's nothing to cover me. And I can't get one because there's no way I'm going to give him any more of a view than he already has.

His head snaps to my eyes, off my bare chest, and he blinks. "Sorry, I heard you yell for help."

I cross my chest with my good arm while my body is buzzing with a strange sensation from him still staring at me. I can't place the feeling, and I'm not sure I enjoy it.

"Get out," I snap at him. He blinks once, then twice. "I thought you were Kelsey," I say. He blinks again and then closes his eyes, turning to the door.

"What are you doing here anyway?"

His back is still facing me when he drops his head and stares at his feet. "I decided to take the day off today. I thought we could talk."

I puff out a breath, frustrated. "Kelsey's coming over to talk to me."

"Hey, sexy girl! I brought your breakfast!" I shriek as Kelsey's loud, hyper voice and face make an appearance in the doorway. I blush, again, at someone else seeing me naked and spread out in the bathtub. "Oh . . ." she says when she sees me, over Adam's shoulder, in the tub. She flicks her eyes back to the living room. "Do you want me to go?"

Her eyebrows are raised in question and there's a slight hint of a blush on her cheeks. I can only imagine what she thinks she just walked in on.

"No," I say firmly. "I need your help getting out, though. I forgot a towel." And I need her to shave the armpit I can't reach, but I'm not saying that with Adam still in the doorway.

Adam takes a step out of the bathroom and Kelsey's hand goes to his shoulder. She shoots him a sympathetic glance, but he shakes his head and leaves the room.

"I need you to help me shave, too," I finally say once she's in the bathroom with two towels stacked on the floor outside the tub.

She nods and goes to work, then finishes rinsing the conditioner that I missed out of my hair. Once she helps me climb out of the bathtub and I'm wrapped in two towels, she holds on to my elbow for my support in getting to my bedroom.

It's actually the guest bedroom, but once I was brought back from the hospital to a strange place, I wasn't ready to share a bed with a stranger. Adam offered to use the guest room, but I insisted, not entirely comfortable even sleeping in a bed that I apparently shared with him. The only thing I recognized in the entire apartment was the guest room's bedding. The same bedding I used in my college apartment with Kelsey.

"He would help you, you know," Kelsey says softly once I'm dressed in a pair of cutoff sweat shorts and a tank top.

"I can't. I don't even know him, and the things I do . . ." I let the words fall and shake my head. "How am I supposed to trust him and let him have his hands all over me?" I flip my hair over, drying it with a towel before tossing it up into a messy bun.

Kelsey nods her head but smiles sadly. "I hope you remember everything soon. You and Adam really are perfect together. I hate seeing both of you so sad."

"Do you know him well?"

Kelsey smirks. "You've been dating him for two years, Amy. Of course I know him well." She wraps me into her arms, squeezing me tightly, and I fight back the instant burning in my eyes. "Do you think I would have been okay with you coming back here if I didn't know how much he loves you and wants to be with you?"

Something flashes across her eyes when she pulls back, but I'm not given an opportunity to ask what else she's thinking before I'm ushered into the kitchen where our bagels are waiting.

We dive into our food silently. I hate that Adam's presence in the apartment ruins any chance for Kelsey to answer every question I have.

THREE

"Can we go somewhere and talk?"

Adam's voice makes me jump and my hands splash in the soapy water. It flies in my face and soaks my T-shirt. I look down and watch the water puddle all over the floor at my feet.

"Shit, I didn't mean to scare you." He immediately grabs a towel and starts wiping the floor. "Don't move," he says quietly, bent down at my feet. "I don't want you to slip and fall."

My heart is beating faster than normal and I feel my hands ball into fists in the water. "No big deal. You just startled me." I pull the drain on the sink and shake the water off my hands, watching the water swirl down the drain and trying to slow down my heart rate.

"So can I take you somewhere?" he asks, but this time his tone is a little more cautious. His hands wring the towel over the sink and I have to take a couple of steps back so he doesn't touch me. If he notices this time, he doesn't show it.

"Where?"

He shrugs and a hint of a smile teases his lips. "Just to campus. I want to show you something."

There's a sparkle in his light brown eyes that I haven't seen before and it intrigues me. Something about it makes me want to say yes.

"Is this about what Dr. Jamison said the other day?"

He nods and sets the towel on the counter, folding it mind-lessly. "I have a feeling you won't trust anything I tell you, but I think it will help if I show you something."

Something inside me cringes at his words and my eyes narrow. Is it the thought of going somewhere with him that makes me nervous? Or is it the thought of not trusting him that I don't like?

I give him a funny look when he turns to me. "It's the mid-dle of campus, Amy. Just come with me." One of his hands runs through his hair, and I watch the muscles in his forearm bend and curve with the movement, almost like they're dancing . . . like his eyes right now.

I can't stop the smile that forms. "Okay." And then I blurt out, "You seem nicer today."

Heat instantly suffuses my cheeks as Adam laughs at me. His voice is low and I feel a pinch in my stomach at his deep, soft rum-ble. He shakes his head, but it's not the same shake he does when he's frustrated with me. "I'm trying to be more understanding about all of this. It's hard for you, I know. You've lost the last two years of college—of your life—and I know you feel lost and con-fused and angry. But it's hard for me, too, to see you go through all of this and not trust me to help you." He pauses and I follow his eyes that wander to the pictures on the wall.

It's a huge mural of photos of us. They're all different-sized black-and-white pictures with black frames. It looks like it catalogs our relationship, and some days when Adam's at work, I stare at the photos, willing myself to remember something. Anything.

But like always, I draw a complete blank.

We're silent for a few minutes, both of us staring at the photos, when he finally speaks. "I love you, and I just want to show you something. Please?"

I turn my eyes to him but he's still staring at the wall, no emotion on his face. He gives none of his thoughts away, and I go back to staring at the pictures, too, wondering when any of them will make sense to me.

~

We're on a large, grassy area that is surrounded by a maze of sidewalks halfway between the main library on campus and the business building. A sense of calm has filled me ever since we arrived on campus. I may not remember anything of the last two years, but for the two years before my missing memories, this place was my home. I practically lived in these two large buildings either studying at the library or going to class at the business building.

The air has a slight chill to it, so I graciously take Adam's zip-up sweatshirt when he offers it to me.

I zip it up, lean against a tree, and smile at my surroundings while memories flash through my mind. As a freshman, Kelsey and I both went through sorority rush week. It took me about two days to realize I didn't want anything to do with that scene, but Kelsey loved it. I dropped out, while she finished and joined the Gamma Beta house. It was the first time in our friendship that I was worried we would drift apart. We haven't, at least not that I'm aware of, but I remember being nervous that everything would change after she was immediately welcomed into the arms of forty new "sisters."

Attending Denver University was a huge issue with my parents. It wasn't nearly as pretentious a school as my parents wanted me to attend. They would have preferred I went somewhere out West—Stanford, mainly—but I dug my heels in, not wanting to leave Colorado, and chose the most prominent private college in Denver. I would have preferred going to a simple state school, but after months of arguing during my junior year of high school, this was the only compromise they were willing to make.

"What are you thinking about?" Adam asks, sitting down next to me. He's close but there's space between us and he looks uncomfortable. I wonder if it's because there's distance between us or if he's worried about what I'm thinking.

I shrug, looking out at the doors to the library and squinting my eyes against the sun. "My parents. I was just thinking about how I had to argue with them to get them to allow me to come here."

Out of the corner of my eye, I see a small smile appear on his lips.

"Why does that make you happy?" I ask, turning to him. His smile drops, but I can tell he wants to say something. "You don't like my parents, do you?"

He runs his hands through his hair and I take him in. His cheeks and chin are scruffy and his bottom lip is fuller than his top. I watch as he sucks his top lip between his teeth, debating what to say.

"Whether or not I like them doesn't matter, Amy. They're your parents." He leans back, resting on the palms of his hands, and crosses his flip-flopped feet at the ankles.

"But you don't like them," I say, urging him on. "I may not know much, Adam, but if I'm going to remember anything, I think I should be able to have honest conversations with you."

He watches me for a minute. His eyes don't drift from mine, but it feels as if he's evaluating me, seeing me in a way that no one else has ever seen me. "No, I don't like them." I watch him, patiently, and wait for him to continue. "I think that no matter what you do, they will always be disappointed in you, and it pisses me off. You're intelligent and beautiful, kind and compassionate, but the only thing they care about is how you live up to their standards and what they want for you. They never stop to think about what you want and what will make you happy, only what will make them look good at the country club and in the press."

My mouth drops open a little bit. I'm stunned at how well he has my parents nailed. He has just said everything I have thought since I turned fourteen and adamantly refused to go through another year of ballet.

I take a minute to process what this means, that Adam knows my parents and their opinions of me so well. The frustration I always feel when I talk to him begins to simmer inside me. All of the answers I get only lead to more questions.

With my eyebrows knitted together, I pull away from his gaze and look back to the library. "So why did you bring me here?"

Adam scoots up, sitting cross-legged like me so we're sitting next to each other. His knee brushes mine and I flinch, and then relax, feeling uneasy that I'm touching a stranger, but maybe too nervous to pull away and see the disappointment or anger in him. His hands are still behind him, propping him up as he looks out at the lawn and the library stairs.

"This is where I saw you for the first time," he finally says, his voice low and uncertain.

If Adam notices my heartbeat pick up, beating a rhythmic drumming sound in my ears, he doesn't mention it.

He points a finger at the library stairs. "You were coming out of the doorway right there," he starts, then drags his finger to the left side of the lawn. "I was over there, kicking the soccer ball around with some guys from the team during a break from our classes." My eyes drift to the two places that aren't very far apart from each other. "You skipped down the stairs, and then once you reached the bottom, you threw your arms and legs around some blond guy and you laughed."

I push my eyebrows together and press my lips together. Tyler? That can't be.

"You laughed so loud and sounded so happy that I was distracted. When Zander kicked the ball to me, it hit me in the side of the head and bounced to the sidewalk, landing almost at your feet."

I gasp and turn to him. "That was you?" I remember everything he's telling me. But that can't be. From what I've been told, Adam and I didn't start dating until October of my junior year. I dated Tyler my sophomore year. Tyler met me at the library after I was done studying for my Finance 250 final. He had just found out he passed his biochem midterm. He had been so worried about finding out his grade, not wanting to ruin his straight-A average. I was so happy for him that when the ball landed at my feet, I kicked it as hard as I could, sailing the ball over some guy who was on his knees on the grass and to the group of guys behind him who were laughing their heads off.

Adam smiles at me, watching the memory play out in my head. Two days after that, I found out Tyler cheated on me at a frat party with a girl from Kelsey's sorority house. Kelsey didn't waste any time telling me, and I broke up with Tyler immediately. I wasn't that upset. Our families ran in the same social circles and when my mom encouraged me to date him, I did it just to get her off my back. When we dated, I never felt anything more than a decent friendship. I mostly stayed with him because it kept my parents happy. The next weekend, I saw Tyler on campus with a bloody lip and smiled to myself when I passed him with a simple "hello." I figured he got caught sticking his tongue in the wrong girl's mouth and her boyfriend didn't like it too much.

A hint of pink blossoms on Adam's cheek as I stare at him, as if he's embarrassed or nervous at what I'm thinking. "You were the guy on the grass?" I ask, with a slight twinge of humor in my voice.

"You took my breath away that day. I didn't even know who you were, and I knew you had a boyfriend, but you seemed so beautiful when you laughed and then when you threw your arms around Tyler, I wanted to find out more about you."

"And you did?" I ask, confused. This was still months before Adam and I met.

He shrugs unashamedly. "I heard about you from some girls in the Gamma house at a party we had one night at our house, but that was after . . ." His voice trails off, but a darkness flickers across his brown eyes. I don't miss the anger that quickly appears and then vanishes just as fast.

"After Tyler cheated on me," I finish for him. His hands press into the grass and his body goes tight. I gasp again, my eyes wide. "You beat him up for me? Why would you do that?"

"Because it takes a special sort of entitled asshole to think he can cheat on his girl and get away with it. I wanted to teach him that he wasn't worth shit when he walked around thinking the world owed him something special just because he existed."

"So it was to bring down a spoiled rich boy and had nothing to do with me." Tyler never meant that much to begin with and I wasn't all that brokenhearted when we broke up, but for a stranger to beat him up for my honor? Who does that?

"It had everything to do with you." Adam's voice is quiet and he stares out at the library stairs as if he's mentally re-creating the first day he saw me. His statement makes my pulse quicken, and I press my hands together, rubbing my fingers so he doesn't see them tremble.

"But you didn't talk to me then, even after you knew we broke up."

Out of the corner of my eye, Adam shakes his head. "No, it was almost summer break and I had to go home. I figured I'd try to find you again when school started back up in the fall."

"And did you?" But I already know the answer, because apparently, we're together. I just don't remember how it happened.

"The very first week." His voice is almost a whisper and sends a shiver of nerves—or excitement—through me. I'm not ready to find out which.

"But you told me we didn't start dating until October."

"You made me work for it." He smirks and I want to ask him what he's remembering. I can only imagine. From what I can tell, we're completely different people. I grew up in a financially privileged home, while it doesn't seem like he did. I was raised to be snotty and pretentious, and while I've always tried hard to fight it, I had a bad tendency to judge people before I knew them, my first year of college. I worked hard to change it, to step away from my family and be my own person, but when your parents pay for everything and run your life, there is little leeway with breaking from the reins.

Something in my gut tells me that meeting Adam snapped in half the reins my parents held, and they don't like it very much.

"Where is your home?" I have been told very little about Adam. There are no pictures of anyone in his family on our black-and-white photo mural. I also haven't asked any questions.

"Iowa." That's all I get. I turn to Adam when he's silent for too long, and all I see in his eyes is a coldness that would chill the strongest of men to their bones.

∽

We're sitting in the library, tucked into the back corner on the fourth floor where the special collections are kept. I love studying back here because it's completely quiet. It's my favorite place to study, but trying to help Adam with his statistics homework in such a private place is dizzying.

No man has ever affected me the way he does with his light brown eyes that seem to unravel every thought I have before it's spoken, and his strong fingers that perhaps not-so-accidentally brush against my arm or my thigh while I'm explaining the concept of linear regression.

I laugh at whatever it was he just said and shake my head once, giving him a frustrated smile. "I'm not helping you in order to get a date. I hear you have plenty."

One side of his lips twitches. "I don't date, Amy. I don't need to."

Right. Because Adam is sex on a stick and most of the girls on campus are willing to jump into his bed without being asked.

"Then you won't be hurt when I tell you no. Again."

"I may never recover." His eyes darken and my belly does that flip-flop thing it's been doing for the last few weeks when he brushes up against me. I blink, trying to clear my thoughts and regain my sanity, but when I do, Adam's hand is no longer holding his pencil on the table. Instead, his hand is brushing away a lock of my brown hair and the other rests on the back of my neck, playing with my hair and pulling me forward.

My breath hitches just as his lips are inches from me. I freeze, putting pressure on his hand to stop the forward movement.

His eyes sparkle in mischief.

"What are you doing?"

His tongue darts out, sucking lightly on his top lip, making it almost disappear. He laughs. I blush, knowing he just watched me check out his mouth. Kissed his mouth with my eyes alone.

"I'm going to kiss you, Ames. And then you're going to finally agree to a date with me."

"One kiss and I'll be unable to resist you? Is that your plan?"

"Sounds like a good plan to me."

I bet his kisses leave a girl gasping for breath and throwing her morals to the floor along with her clothes.

He wipes the smirk off my lips by lightly brushing his lips once, and then twice, against mine. I instantly know why every girl wants to get *her hands on him and his hands in her pants. My body lights up like a wildfire as he presses his lips against mine more firmly, taking what he wants and expecting me to give in. God, I want to give in, to just once in my life go for what it is that I want and not what I'm told is best for me.*

And I'm just about to throw away all my fears about him. I twist my hands that were frozen on the table out from underneath his arms and place them on his thighs. His muscular legs tighten and his lips turn into a slight smile against mine.

"Adam? Are you up here?"

The shrill sound of a high-pitched voice is like a bucket of cold water dumped on my head, and I jerk back away from him.

His eyes are still closed and I was right. I'm gasping for breath.

I press my lips together to stop my lower lip from trembling. How could I be so stupid to finally give in to him? I'm just a chase, a challenge. I just let him have what he's been trying to get for weeks. And I handed it over so easily.

Adam frowns when he opens his eyes, right as the girl comes around the corner and sees us sitting way too close together to be studying. Never mind the fact that we're both breathing heavily.

Shame fills me. Not only for kissing Adam, but for giving in to the man who already has his afternoon sex appointment showing up.

"There you are." The girl smiles at me in a way that says she knows I'm no competition for her. I sit back, clumsily gathering my notebook and textbook into my backpack. "I was wondering if you forgot about me."

Adam drops his head before turning to her, and I see his smile out of the corner of my eye. The same one he just gave to me. The same one that says he can have everything and anything he wants.

"Of course I didn't forget, Lexi. I was just running late."

He says it calmly, like he's completely unaffected by the kiss we just shared.

I want to kick my own shins at my stupidity. I deserve it. I need someone to knock some sense into me. It obviously flees to the dark corners of the room whenever Adam is around.

I stand up, throwing my bag over one shoulder, anxious to get away from him. Away from him and Lexi together, knowing what they'll be doing in about five minutes in these private, hidden corners. "Right. Well, I'll, uh . . . I'll see you in class, then."

I don't look at him as I start to walk away, but he grabs my wrist and tugs on it so I have no choice but to stop and look down at him. He's still sitting in the chair, grinning like he doesn't have a care in the world.

"Why are you running?"

I look to him and Lexi. She's a cheerleader for the football team and on the soccer team's pep squad. She probably spends hours lusting after Adam, watching him running up and down the soccer field. Shirtless. Sweaty.

"You have plans."

He shakes his head and frowns. "She can wait a few minutes. We weren't done here."

Lexi is standing behind him with her arms crossed, letting me know that she very well can't wait a few minutes. "Adam." He looks at Lexi but keeps a hold of my hand. "We really need to go."

He tugs on my hand and smiles that same damn smile. This time it doesn't work on me.

"We are done here." By the tone in my voice he knows I'm not just talking about the tutoring. I pull my hand out of his and I'm at the end of the long aisle stacked with books all the way to the ceiling when he calls my name.

Against my better judgment, which has always led me on the straight path in the past, I turn back to him. He has his book loosely held in one hand at his side, the other draped around Lexi's shoulder.

She leans into him and he doesn't pull her hand away when she lightly wipes it across his chest, giggling. She giggles. In what universe is a giggling twentysomething attractive?

"I'll get my date one way or another." He winks and they disappear.

~

Silence filled our apartment for the entire weekend after I asked about Adam's parents when we were on campus. His eyes went cold, every muscle tightened, and when he declared it was time to go, I was already packing up the picnic, knowing that our walk down his memory lane was over. He's frustrating and his ability to shut down his emotions so quickly scares me as we try to maneuver around each other in the small apartment.

I felt like we were beginning to take a small step forward. I remembered seeing him the very first time, even if I didn't know it was him. But as I sift through the memory of that day outside the library, and then the reminder of seeing Tyler's black eye . . . I knew he was being honest. It made me hopeful that I could begin to trust him to help me through this. But his ability to shut down so quickly afterward felt like a slap in my face. Why won't he answer questions about his parents? Or anything about himself? Besides the pictures on the wall, I know nothing about him and he doesn't offer up much.

And every time I dream of him, he's got his arms wrapped around another girl while flirting with me. None of it makes sense.

I spent all week, while Adam was at work as an intern with a custom-home-building company, tossing around the idea of moving back home. But live with my parents again? It's the only place I have to go, and I spent the first eighteen years of my life counting down the days to get out of there.

Regardless of my uncertainty, every time I've gone into our closet to grab my suitcase and pack up—to leave and get out before Adam knows I'm considering it—I stop.

Something continually tells me that staying in this apartment with Adam is the only way to get answers, regardless of how uncomfortable it makes me.

FOUR

Dr. Jamison ushers us into her office five minutes late, and we take our standard seats on the opposite side of her desk.

I begin filling her in about the assignment she gave me. Adam fidgets next to me the entire time while I repeat what he showed me, and what I remember, about the first time he saw me.

"So what did you think of what Adam showed you?" she finally asks when I'm done.

I shrug. "It was nice. I mean, I don't remember meeting him, and I didn't know he was the guy on the ground at the time, but I knew it happened as soon as he told me."

"And did it help you trust him?"

Next to me, Adam nervously wipes his hands on his thighs. My fingers play with my messy bun piled on the top of my head.

"It did," I start hesitantly, and then remember the dream of the second girl, and my hands drop into my lap.

"But what?"

I turn to Adam, and for the first time hate all the uncertainty between him and me. It's all twisted together like an elaborate spider web, and I'm caught with no way out.

"What is it, Amy?" Dr. Jamison's voice shakes me out of my thoughts. I sigh.

"He's always with a girl. Always. Whenever I dream, there's always someone else that has his attention."

I look away at the empty playground out the window and feel just as lonely and abandoned as the rickety metal swings that never seem to get any attention.

"I can't take back my history, Ames." I close my eyes at his nickname for me. Every time he says it, I cringe, knowing it speaks of an intimacy we have that I don't remember. "But I never cheated on you."

The confidence in his voice makes me turn to him. His black hair is just long enough that it flips out over the sides of his ears; his chin and cheeks sport at least a day's worth of growth. His eyes seem to pull me in, even when I try to look away from him.

I try to take him in just as he is, to move past this lost feeling and remember what he told me on the college campus. He looks the same as he did then, with such sincerity and honesty as he told me about the first time he saw me.

I smile at the thought. I did trust him. I believed him. Maybe it will help me trust him more with what he says to me in the future.

"Okay," I whisper, but I feel something soften in me. Maybe I really did trust Adam and love him like everyone says. Maybe I just need to get to know him more and everything else will begin to make more sense.

Dr. J. scribbles something in her notebook, allowing Adam and me this moment, however small it is, to savor a success.

∾

"Favorite color?"

He flashes me a strange look as he pulls out of the parking lot. "I just need answers."

He pulls his eyebrows together for a second and then nods. "Blue, like your eyes."

I press my lips together, hoping it will keep the blush away from my cheeks.

"Favorite band?"

He nods toward the car stereo. I don't recognize the music, but I like it even if it's different than the pop and dance music I normally listen to. Or did, I think, as I remember all the band T-shirts hanging in my closet.

"Radiohead. We saw them in concert last year when they came to Colorado Springs." His eyes go hazy like he's remembering something, but I don't ask. I don't want to remember anything, or try to force myself today. I just want to see what it is we have in common. Why we're together.

"Favorite place to visit?"

His smile fades and his eyes darken, but then he turns to me. "The cliffs."

I don't want to ask why his favorite place makes him sad. I tip my lips into a slight smile. "That's *my* favorite place to go." I found these secluded hiking cliffs when I was sixteen years old. Kelsey and I went there all the time. On the other side of the cliffs were these gorgeous waterfalls that Kelsey and I always talked about jumping off but were never brave enough to try.

He licks his bottom lip and smiles at me. "I know."

I clear my throat. "Favorite memory?"

"That's easy," he says, and pulls the car to a stop outside our apartment building. He turns to me and picks up my hand. His thumb softly rubs against my knuckles, watching my eyes to see if I'm going to pull away, but I can't. My arm sent sparks of fire through my entire body as soon as he touched me. I feel this burning sensation inside of me that, for the first time, I know isn't fear.

It's attraction. It makes me uneasy and nervous, in a good way, at the same time. "The day you said yes."

"Said yes to what?" My voice sounds scratchy. How is a simple thumb on my knuckles making my knees shake together?

Adam leans over and presses his lips gently against my hand. I pull back, but he holds on tighter, smiling lightly and still looking at me. "To all of it."

And then he gets out of the car and opens my door. I don't know how long I sit there, still staring at the spot on my hand, waiting for the fire to stop burning.

Finally, I face him without getting out of the car. He frowns and holds his hand out to help me, but I shake my head.

"Take me to all the places we used to go."

~

Martino's Pizzeria is just a few blocks off campus. It's a small restaurant with an outdoor deck, and the inside is bright and modern; not the usual red-and-white-checkered tablecloth kind of pizza place. I like it immediately. Adam insists we order the MJ Special and gyro pizzas, but I eye both of them warily when the beautiful waitress sets them down in front of us. Her black hair is pulled into a low ponytail that falls almost to her waist and she has the most exotic features of anyone I've ever seen.

"Thank you, Megan." My eyes bounce back and forth between Adam and the waitress, and then I frown.

She offers us a friendly smile. "You're welcome, Adam." She turns to me and places her hand on my shoulder. Her voice is soft but kind. "It's nice to see you, Amy. We were all worried about you."

And then she walks away. I stare at her dumbfounded until she passes through the door to the kitchen.

"I know her?"

Adam smiles and bites into the gyro pizza. Spiced lamb meat sounds, well, like something that shouldn't be on a pizza in my opinion, but he insists I like it. "We come here a lot. She and her husband own the place. They're pretty cool."

"Gyro meat?" I ask again as I pick up a small slice with a crispy thin crust.

"Just try it."

I take a bite and moan, instantly. Oh my gah—it's like the best thing I've ever had in my entire life.

By the time I'm full, we've not only finished off both pizzas, but also devoured their peach dessert pizza. Dessert pizza? I might have to have it every day. And it has fresh fruit on it—so it's healthful.

When we walk up to pay, a guy with spiky blond hair comes out from the kitchen, wiping his hands on a black apron wrapped around his waist. He walks right up to us and clasps Adam on the shoulder with one hand and shakes his hand with the other.

"Good to see you, man. It's been a while."

Adam agrees and then lifts his hand out to the side, introducing me. "You remember Amy. Amy, this is Joe, the owner."

I offer up my hand to shake, but I'm enveloped into a large, warm hug with my hand captured in between us. My other arm falls limply to my side and I shoot Adam a wide-eyed look. "It's good to see you're doing okay, Amy," Joe says when he pulls back.

"Thank you," I mumble, slightly uncomfortable with the fact that I don't know these people. Adam puts his hand on my lower back and I let him, but I still flinch slightly.

When Adam offers up his credit card to pay, Joe waves him off. "It's on the house. We just hope we'll be seeing our favorite customers around here more often."

My eyes take in the restaurant while Adam and Joe make a little bit of small talk that I completely tune out.

From the corner of my eye, I catch something small shimmering from the ceiling in a corner booth. It looks like one of those wind catcher things I used to make in arts and crafts when I was a little girl, and before I know it, I'm standing directly under it.

It's a small cluster of butterflies, and their metal outlines seem as fragile as the real-life thing. I watch their wings moving slowly, probably drifting from the current of the air-conditioning. I can't do anything but watch them, and I don't know why.

But suddenly, playing in my mind like any other memory, it's there. Visible.

I'm sitting in the booth, and Adam's arm is around me. His thumb is making small circles on my bare shoulder and he wipes away a tear with his other thumb. I shake my head, upset and sad at the same time. I close my eyes, tipping my head back against the booth as Adam holds me. We don't say anything, but when I open my eyes—I see them. The butterflies. A half dozen of them are swaying gently through the air. They look like a mixture of silver and diamonds and so real. So lifelike. So free.

"I want to be like them," I say quietly, not moving my eyes from the butterflies. "I want to be free."

"Amy?" I jump at the sound of Adam's voice. He has his hand out like he's about to touch my shoulder, but I pull back, out of his reach. A memory. My first memory while I was awake. I look up at the butterflies and they still seem so real. Just like I remembered.

"We sat here."

Adam looks to the booth where I had seen us sitting, him comforting me.

He nods, seeming unsure of what to do or what to say. Was that real? I'm sure it was. I know it was by the way Adam is looking at me—full of hope and yet fear at the same time.

"Yeah, we did," he finally says, but I'm not looking at him. I can't take my eyes off those butterflies. *I want to be free.*

Free of what?

"I'm tired." I feel a pressure on my temples that wasn't there moments ago, along with a dull throbbing in my ankle signaling I've been on my feet for too long today. Maybe this was too much of a trip down memory lane for me to handle.

I remembered something. Good or bad, I don't know, but it's a start. As I finally climb under my covers once we get home, it gives me hope.

FIVE

Kelsey and I are sitting next to each other in the reception room at the Little Mountain Country Club. We're dressed like it's high school prom all over again. She's wearing a dress that's deep red and falls to her ankles but has a slit on one side that goes up to her mid-thigh. When she crosses her legs, you can see a flash of her garter belt. Zander licks his lips every time he sees it. The color is stunning on her with her porcelain skin and waist-long brown hair. Some people used to confuse Kelsey and me for sisters because our hair color and length is almost the same, but we've always thought that's where the similarities end. Her eyes are a pale blue—so light they almost look clear—while mine are dark like the ocean in the midst of a hurricane. My olive skin color makes me look like I always have a slight tan.

Adam hasn't taken his hands off my dark-gray silk dress all night. Its length and thigh slit are similar to Kelsey's, but my dress is held up by thin shoulder straps. The back comes down to my waist, and the front is cut so low it dips down into my cleavage. It's the most risqué thing I've ever chosen to wear in my life. I was so nervous while I was getting ready that I thought I was going to throw up, but as soon as Adam saw it and almost went cross-eyed staring at me, I knew I made the right choice.

He has had a hand touching me all night long and it's keeping me right at the breaking point of wanting to take him back to his place so we can be alone versus wanting him so badly I almost jumped him in *the limo we shared with four other couples on our way to their fraternity's winter formal.*

And even though I'm thankful Adam has let me set the pace, I don't think my heart can take waiting anymore. I love him and I want to show him how much.

My mind races, wondering what it's going to be like. His body is so strong, but he's always been so gentle with me. A simple kiss from Adam leaves me panting, my mouth dry, and my body starving, clawing at him for more. I take anything he gives me because as soon as Adam touches me, my brain turns to a gooey mess, unable to think about anything except the heat my body absorbs from him.

"What is it, Ames?" Adam whispers in my ear quietly enough so no one else at the table can hear.

"Huh?" His hand moves higher on my thigh and squeezes. I look down, and then to his eyes, and blush. My body shivers, imagining the fire that will be lit when he's inside of me.

"You've been acting nervous all night. What's going on?" The line between Adam's eyes deepens and I hear him grind his teeth together. I look across the table, glancing at Adam's fraternity brother and his date, Britnee. She's had Adam before and she's made it no secret that she wants more of him. I don't necessarily blame her. Adam's fingers are like a drug; his kisses, the strongest heroin possible.

I shake my head, clearing the doubts of Britnee from my mind, and focus on Adam, where everything always becomes clear. My fingers go up and play with the hair at the nape his neck, one fingernail lightly scratching his stubble in front of his ear. I love that he always has a bit of roughness to him. The burn from his scratchy chin and cheeks always leaves a reminder that he's been with me, even after he's gone.

"I want . . . more, Adam." I've always been confident and proud of who I am. I am comfortable in my skin, but Adam has a way of making me rethink everything I've been taught and believed in my entire life. It's as exciting as it is unsettling.

I feel Adam's other hand slide to the back of my neck and he pulls me close. I refuse to look at anyone else, afraid people will be gawking at us in such an intimate position at the table in front of his closest fifty fraternity brothers.

His breath sends shivers down my spine and leaves a pool of heat in my lap as his lips brush lightly against my ear. "Are you telling me what I think you're telling me?"

I can only nod.

"Because I want you, Amy. I want to know what it feels like to sink inside of you and feel every part of you against me, but I need you to be sure." He pulls back slightly. Our noses are almost touching. He's so close I have to blink so I can see both of his eyes instead of one blurry one.

"I just need a minute." I stand quickly and scurry off to the bathroom before I can embarrass myself at the table.

I'm running cold water over my wrists when Kelsey walks into the bathroom. She crosses her arms and leans against the wall.

"What was that about?"

I wipe my hands on a paper towel, too afraid to look at her. She's been pushing me toward Adam for months. I can't tell if it's because she's dating Zander and likes it when we can all go out, or if she really thinks he's good for me. But whenever I doubt myself or Adam, she's always been there to push me to have fun and let everything else go.

"I can't do it, Kels." I shake my head and laugh. She knew my plans for the night. She could tell by how nervous I was when we got ready together in our apartment. She handed me a strip of condoms and told me to get some.

"Fine," she says, throwing her arms up in the air. "Do what you want, but you really need to get over the fact that Adam was a man-whore before you. He's not anymore, and he's not using you. Have sex with him or not, but either way, he's not going to pressure you and he's not going anywhere."

She leaves, letting the bathroom door slam behind her. I can only *laugh. Kelsey's trust is hard to earn, yet she seems to understand Adam more than I do.*

Adam never stays with anyone for long, and while I've tried to mentally keep my distance from him, my heart has never once received the message. It's gone forward, full speed ahead, and fallen completely in love with the unattainable sex god of Denver U.

Admitting it to myself silently in the mirror, I feel my pulse quicken and make a decision to, for once in my life, follow my heart. I will worry about healing my heart when it breaks and not a minute before.

"You can do this," I tell myself in the mirror.

I shake my head again, feeling foolish for talking to myself in the mirror, and go back to find Adam. To tell him I'm sure. To tell him that I want him. I want to feel his hands all over every part of me.

But as soon as I open the door to the bathroom, I want to take back every good thought I've ever had about him.

Because plastered against the wall in the hallway is Britnee, and Adam is the one doing the plastering. Every single inch of his long frame pushes against her. She has a fist holding his tie between them and his hands are against the brick wall, his lips pressed against hers . . . moving.

I stand there, frozen. Unable to move, unable to speak, and unable to scream that he's the biggest fucking asshole in the whole world.

Why?

Because I knew this would happen going into it. I knew this would happen from the day he asked me to tutor him in statistics. My damn, stupid, romantic heart thinking he would change for me—because of me—is the only idiot. My head knew he would never change.

As if she knew to expect me, Britnee pushes him back but keeps a fist around his tie. I want to break that hand with its acrylic French-manicured nails. Slowly. Ripping every single one off and taking her real nail in the process.

Adam jumps back and spins around to face me. "I was just coming to check on you." He takes the back of his hand and wipes his mouth, smearing her hot pink hooker lipstick all over his mouth and his hand.

"Seems like you got sidetracked." My voice is cold, unforgiving, and Adam flinches at my tone.

"It's not what you think. She just grabbed me." He turns to Britnee, who is still smiling at me with her back against the wall. One hand is still wrapped around Adam's forearm, and he yanks it off his arm, throwing her hand down. He glares at her quickly before his eyes return to mine.

I roll my shoulders back and hold my head high, because I don't need him. I don't need anyone. I push past him in the hallway. He will not humiliate me. I'm a Thompson, and we don't get humiliated. We're better than that. I'm better than him.

The thought shocks me. For once, I agree with my mom. I am better than him.

"Amy, wait." I know he's following me, but I don't stop. I grab my clutch and my cell phone from the table without missing a step. I get to the doorway that leads outside, when I suddenly see Brendan. He's an asshole. He's on the football team and thinks every guy should kiss his feet and every girl should suck his dick just because he can throw a ball made from a murdered pig. He's hit on me more times than I can count in the last two years.

Before I can think about what I'm doing, my hands are clasped behind his neck and his lips are mine. He grunts and his eyes fly wide open at first, but because he's that big of a dick, he quickly takes control. His tongue pushes into my mouth and I have to swallow down the bile in my throat. He reeks of beer. I don't care and I don't let it stop me.

I can feel the first crack of heartache hit my chest as Brendan pulls me to him, his erection tight in his tuxedo pants.

"What the fuck!" Adam yells.

One second Brendan's lips are on mine, and the next, I'm staring into Adam's feral-looking eyes. He's pissed? I just caught him kissing the easiest girl on campus.

Behind him, Britnee is pulling on Adam's arm, even as he's trying to shake her off.

Every eye in the country club is on us and it gives me courage to do what needs to be done. My blood turns to ice in my veins, and I temporarily push down all the pain I feel.

I will not be played a fool. Not by Britnee and not by Adam.

"Sorry, Adam. It's been fun." His jaw drops open and his hands tighten into fists.

Britnee stands next to him, just as wide-eyed, but with excitement and victory. She's getting what she wanted. I'm handing him to her. She should thank me, really.

I turn to Brendan, who looks a bit stunned, like he just realized what's happening and who he was just kissing in front of his entire frat house. Adam and Brendan have never gotten along, and I've never cared to ask why. I don't care now. I just need an escape, and he's the perfect guy to give me one.

I pull on his tie, lightly, and he looks down at me. "Take me home."

I don't even know if he has a date. If he does, he doesn't seem to care as his eyes go hazy and he pulls his car keys out of his front pocket.

"Don't do this, Amy. I didn't do anything wrong." I don't look at Adam, too afraid of what I'll see, but then I decide I'm stronger than this. I'm stronger than him.

"We both knew it wouldn't last, right?" My voice sounds scarily haunting, and he flinches again. "Remember? You told me yourself."

Without another word, I turn away from Adam, pulling Brendan out the front door of the country club. Brendan has a cocky grin on his face and he follows me willingly. Excitedly.

No one else follows me. No one stops me; not even Kelsey.

~

I have begun slowly remembering things after that day in Martino's. Last week I walked past a music store and picked up a Coldplay album. I stood in the middle of the store and it felt like the album jumped into my hands—like I was meant to own it.

I bought it because the feeling to possess it was so strong, even if I didn't understand. It wasn't until I was walking home that I remembered the concert T-shirt collection in my closet and had a flash of standing with Adam in a sea of people watching the same band sing a song that I knew was called "In My Place." I went back to the apartment and grabbed my iPod, not surprised at all to see it filled with rock albums that were vaguely familiar, and yet I knew every word. I loved every word.

Adam came home from work and found me sitting on the living room floor, surrounded by albums and T-shirts that all went together. He said nothing as he sat down on the floor and dropped his head against the cushions. We spent three hours listening to music and didn't say a word.

And yet, he had a hint of a smile. Just a slight tilt to his lips that told me he was happy.

I remembered a picnic lunch I had with Kelsey, Zander, and Adam, sitting in the middle of the university grounds, the same place where Adam saw me for the first time. We were drinking sparkling grape juice and eating cheese and crackers, toasting to the end of our spring midterms.

But it all changed with that stupid dream I had four days ago that I'm still unable to get out of my head. I haven't said anything to Adam. I don't ask him. I just pull back. And I know he can tell. I know he notices that every time he sits down on the couch, I move farther away. I know he's pissed, because I can practically hear his teeth grinding from another room. He leaves at night and doesn't come back for hours.

I don't know where he goes and I don't ask. I don't need to. When he comes home at night, I'm already in bed, but I can hear him fumbling with the key in our lock. I hear him stumble through our kitchen, knocking into the chairs and the walls on the way to the bathroom.

Last night he stopped outside my bedroom. My heart rate picked up and started beating wildly against my chest when I heard a low thump hit my door and saw his shadow from the crack underneath it.

I froze and watched the shadow stay still. Minutes passed and there was no movement from outside, no sound at all. I almost thought he passed out in the hallway, but as I got out of bed to check on him, a louder thumping sound hit the wall and I scurried back into bed like a frightened kitten. He let out a string of curse words before he slammed the door to his room and the apartment went silent.

When I woke up, there was a chunk of drywall missing from the wall and half a dozen dark red dots on the carpet.

It only confirms the suspicion I've had in my head all week long, ever since that dream. We were always a disaster waiting to happen. Everything I've seen in the dreams, everything I've felt always leads back to that conclusion. The fear, the uncertainty, the jealousy—never once have I seen, or felt, any redeeming quality from either of us as I remember how we began. We bring out the worst in each other.

SIX

W hat do you think?" I spin around in the three-way mirror. Kelsey watches me with a funny expression. "That bad?"

She wrinkles her nose. "It's been a while since I've seen you in a dress." I frown in the mirror, watching her regard me like I've grown two heads instead of put on a navy-and-white maxi dress. "It looks strange."

"I like it," I say, hands on my hips, convincing myself this should be a part of my new wardrobe. Kelsey looks doubtful. "What's wrong with a dress?"

"Nothing. It's just . . ." she starts, and then sighs, running her hand through her long dark hair. "You just swore you'd never wear a dress again."

I press my teeth together until my jaw hurts. She's had this same attitude for the last three hours. She took me to the hospital for my doctor's appointment, and as soon as my casts were removed, I asked her to bring me shopping. She looks like she's regretted the choice to come with me ever since I tried on my first dress.

Hell, I'm regretting having her with me.

"Yeah, well, I don't remember that," I snap at her, and fling back the curtain in the dressing room.

A minute later, while I'm clad only in my bra and underwear,

Kelsey walks in with a silent apology written all over her face. I ignore her while I pull on my jeans.

"You can't keep throwing fits and being pissy with me for crap like this."

"I know," she mumbles. "Do you remember when you were fourteen and stopped doing ballet in order to play lacrosse?"

"Yes."

Lacrosse looked fun and gave me an excuse to get off the ballet stage, where I was forced to spend hours practicing even though I never liked dance. My mom refused to speak to me for a month, and when she did, the first words out of her mouth were, "You look like a boy with all that muscle."

"Well, the dresses thing was something similar. You ditched them over the winter when you and Adam got serious."

I frown. "I changed who I am for him?" I hate that idea. Did I become *that* girl that is so insecure that she changes everything about herself to become what a guy wants her to be? I can't see me doing that. But what the hell do I know?

"No," she says, smiling sadly. I look at her through the mirror, adjusting my shirt. "It's more like you became who you always wanted to be, and Adam helped you get there. This is like stepping backward in time."

"So why did I change? And how did I become the girl who only dresses in rock concert T-shirts and denim skirts and jeans?"

She rolls her eyes and I resist the urge to slap her. "It's not about the clothes, Amy, and you know it. You never liked who your parents tried to make you be. Adam just held your hand while you fought against them and found yourself. That's all."

I watch her pale blue eyes soften, willing me to believe her. I can't. The girl I've become with Adam is so far apart from the girl I remember being. And everyone refuses to give me straight answers of how I got from point A to Q.

I pick up the dress, along with the others that I threw in the dressing room but haven't tried on yet. "I'm getting them."

～

I'm in the kitchen making a grilled cheese sandwich when Adam finally crawls out of his room for the day. His unshaven facial hair is longer than I've seen it. His dark hair is sticking up in places and matted down in others. His right hand is wrapped in a bandage and there are dots of dried blood on his knuckles seeping through the gauze. His eyes are bloodshot and he doesn't look at me as he walks to the coffee pot. I feel the tension begin to bubble between us, and instinctively, I straighten my back. I can feel his eyes boring into the back of me as he takes in every inch of my exposed skin.

"Nice dress." By the tone in his voice, he hates the dress.

I don't move. I keep my hands on the counter, watching the sandwich cook on the countertop griddle, and press my lips together.

I don't respond to Adam's sneer, but I see him sit down at the kitchen table with his head draped in his hands. The steam from his coffee cup floats upward and disappears into his hands.

Finally, he rubs his hands roughly over his face and takes his first sip.

"Just tell me about the fucking dream, Amy. Tell me what sort of asshole you think I am now." His nose wrinkles, and over the hissing griddle, I hear him grind his teeth together. He doesn't look at me. He doesn't look at anything. He just stares straight ahead with blank, dark eyes at the television mounted on our far wall.

The smell of burning bread snaps me back to the counter, and I swear, flipping the burnt sandwich into the sink before unplugging the griddle.

How do I tell him how it felt to watch him kiss some girl and then throw my tongue down some asshole's throat just because I was pissed?

I was jealous.

I was *emotional*.

I don't remember there ever being a time in my life where my emotions ruled my actions.

It wasn't what Adam did in the dream that terrified me. I've replayed it in my mind a dozen times and I don't actually think he wanted to kiss Britnee. It was my own actions that have shaken me.

It was how I felt. Crazed. Like a lunatic in search of a drug to satisfy an itch that burned deep in my bones.

I don't understand it, and it scares the hell out of me. It wasn't me. Somehow the girl who moved into this apartment is the complete opposite of the girl I remember being.

She's the evil twin driven by emotions. I can see it. I can feel it in the darkest places inside me that I've somehow changed.

"Just tell me, please." He turns to me with begging eyes, and I realize I've just been staring at him. Or through him, because I haven't seen anything. His voice is desperate, his eyes pleading.

I can't resist.

"We were at a formal for your frat. I walked in on Britnee kissing you in the hallway and took off." I swallow slowly. The scene flashes before my eyes, as I remember the feelings of pain and pride fighting for first place as I ran out of that ballroom.

"And made out with Brendan." His voice is cold as he finishes my sentence, and there's a tightness in his jaw. His undamaged hand grips his mug so harshly that his knuckles are white.

"I went home with him and cheated on you," I clarify. I don't know how the dream ended exactly, but I can imagine. With the hormones and emotions flooding me that night, I have no doubt I let Brendan take me somewhere and do whatever he wanted to me—just because I was pissed.

Adam scoffs and shakes his head. "You didn't cheat on me. Although, I wouldn't have blamed you if you did after what you saw with Britnee."

His eyes drift away from me and out to the window. It's not the first time I watch a dream I had play out as a memory in his eyes. I watch his breath pick up, the tic in his jaw, the anger, and then the sadness unfold. Every emotion I experienced in my dream plays out in his eyes and in his facial expressions as I silently watch him.

"That's not the point." I don't think whether I had revenge sex with Brendan *is* the point, although the thought alone makes me shudder and gives me a sick feeling in my stomach.

"Then what is it? I didn't mean to kiss Britnee. She just pulled me to her before I could stop her."

"And you kissed her back. I saw you."

"I was twenty years old and a walking ball of hormones. I had a hard-on all night long from that fucking dress you were wearing. I was stupid, and it took me a second to register what in the hell was happening. But I didn't want her. I wanted you."

He stands up from the table and walks toward me in the kitchen. His nostrils flare and I know what he's thinking about because I'm thinking the same thing. The way his touch felt like fire through my dress. The way I wanted him. The way I wanted his fingers to dig into my skin and pull me into him. God, I felt it all in my dream and even now standing in front of him, I don't understand the physical pull he has on me.

Like I'm drawn to him, whether I want to be or not.

"Tell me what else you remembered, Amy. Tell me what happened in the dream before that part."

My jaw drops and my eyes widen. My pulse begins dancing across my skin as Adam walks up to me. With his hands on both sides of the counter, he's blocked me into our U-shape kitchen and I can't escape. I take a step back until my back hits the wall. The zipper of my dress digs into my skin and I move against it, hating the feel.

I shake my head. "It's too much."

"Too much what?" His eyes drop to my feet and slowly rake up every inch of me. One side of his lips twists into a sneer when he hits my dress at the knee. He hates it. He hates that I'm not being the me he knows, but rather the one I was before. The two sides of me are confusing. One I don't know, and one I remember but I'm not sure I like.

Too much of this, I think. Too much heat and fire. It's explosive and powerful.

It's scary.

It makes me want to jump off a cliff just so I can drown in cold water.

"I can't do this." I hear my own doubt and breathlessness as his eyes pin me against the wall. It doesn't take anything else besides a look of his narrowed eyes that are clearly warring against something to keep me frozen to the wall.

"Do what, Ames? Let yourself feel again?" He takes a step forward, and then another, until he's standing inches in front of me, towering over me. "Heaven forbid you remember what it's like to feel something. That's what it is, isn't it? That's what you're so afraid of. That's why you've gone back to being the ice princess with this stuck-up little dress."

I shake my head, but inside I'm screaming, "Yes!" at the top of my lungs.

I clear my throat. It's dry and scratchy and *feels* like I've been screaming, though I haven't said a word. "Ice princess?"

He laughs softly, just once, and then a finger comes out and barely brushes my yellow shoulder strap. I shiver, not sure if it's because his finger burned my skin or scared me.

"You know what it means." His breath flows over me, caressing me, and my knees shake. His tone is deep. Seductive. Yet dark and twisted at the same time. Like he's seducing me with sin, and something inside me wants it even though I know it could destroy me. "You were the princess. The girl who had it all figured out. Every action perfectly scripted according to the plan your parents wrote for you."

Blood begins to boil under my skin, and yet I can't move away. He's right. He's completely right. I hated my parents for that. I hated never meeting their expectations but trying my hardest anyway. It was a battle I always lost but a war that I never gave up, so determined to make them proud of me. But hearing it from him, in his voice that is dripping with desire, makes me feel angry again.

How dare this man that I don't remember know every single thing about me.

"What scares you is that you're remembering that you're different now. You just don't know how you got here." I look away, but I can feel his eyes on me. All I see is the dust under the fridge and the dried blood on his damaged hand. He's dangerous in more ways than one.

"You don't know anything," I choke out over a grapefruit-sized lump in my throat.

"You're wrong, Amy." God, his voice sounds smooth like butter and as decadent as chocolate. I close my eyes, trying to fight against what my body is feeling. "I know everything. I know every fear you have. I know how strong you were the day you told your parents you didn't want to work at your dad's firm. I know what your skin feels like when you move beneath me and the sounds you make right before you come."

"Stop it," I whisper, my eyes still closed. He's pressing too hard—not with his body—but with his words and the confidence in them.

"What do you want to know, Ames? I'll tell you anything. First kiss? It was in my room at the frat. First date? We went rock climbing. That first time I saw you in statistics? I left and had a hard-on for two weeks. God, I was so excited to see you on that first day of class. I had dreamed of you all summer. And the first time we had sex? I took you to a suite at the Lux, the very same night of that formal, by the way. I couldn't keep my hands off you and I took you against the wall."

He pauses and I think I might die of a heart attack. The things he's saying are revolting. Dark. Intoxicating. He puts one hand up next to my head on the wall. His other hand leaves my shoulder and falls to my waist.

"It was a lot like this," he says, and slightly squeezes his hand at my hip. Why am I not pushing him away? Why do I like the way he touches me despite how much he scares me?

"What do you want from me?" Slowly, I open my eyes and stare up at him. I can see the fight in them; fighting for control, despite wanting to lose it.

"I want you to feel," he whispers against my ear. It sends my skin dancing. I want to roll my shoulders to erase the feeling, but I can't move, so I stand there and take it, holding my breath at the strong sensation. "Stop trying so hard to remember. Stop thinking and just feel. Feel me, Amy. It's what we've always done best."

His head lowers slowly. Never once does he break eye contact with me, and he doesn't wait for my permission as his lips slide across mine. His tongue flicks out, wetting his lips and mine at the same time. When he presses his mouth to mine, sliding his tongue in before I can resist, I just . . . take it. Because ohmigod it's heaven. As soon as his mouth hits mine and his tongue slides inside, I feel like something inside me is reconnecting, even though I still don't know what's been broken in the first place.

It's passion and love and I can feel it. The kiss is soft but power-ful. His tongue knows exactly where to go as each of our mouths move against the other; he knows exactly what I like and how I like it, even though I've never experienced it. I've kissed guys before. I've even had excellent kisses that made my stomach flip-flop and left me wanting more. I've had sweet kisses that made me lean into the man, wrap my hands around a guy's neck, and pop my foot off the ground like in classic romance films.

But this, this is in a whole new realm of kisses.

"God, Amy." He pulls away, panting for breath, and rests his forehead on mine. "I just . . . fuck . . . I just need you."

I catch another glimpse of his bandaged hand right next to my face, remembering the thump of the wall as he cracked a hole in the drywall, and take a deep breath, collecting myself.

"I can't."

I duck out from under his arm and walk past him, not even looking to see if he turns around. "We're a disaster, Adam. You almost broke your hand last night and everything I see tells me that this . . ." I wave my hands frantically in the air, keeping my back to him. "It's just a fucking mess. We're a mess."

"We were twenty and stupid. Our relationship was never per-fect. You can't expect it to be, but there were a lot more good times than bad. You just haven't gotten to the good stuff yet."

I walk out of the apartment after grabbing my purse and the wedge sandals I bought at the mall earlier in the day. The straps are uncomfortable in the heel and dig into my skin, but I bought them to match the yellow dress with the zipper that is still digging uncomfortably into my back. Damn me and my pride for trying to prove Kelsey wrong.

SEVEN

Ten blocks into my walk, my ankle that is still healing begins protesting against the pain of the wedge sandals. I take them off and throw them in the nearest garbage can. I have no idea how long I walk after that, wandering aimlessly around Denver in nothing but bare feet and a summer dress that's too lightweight for the weather.

By the time the sun begins to set, I'm in a park I don't recognize with a dead cell phone and no idea how to get back to the apartment. Not that I'm sure I want to.

I can still see his amber-colored eyes flashing with desire. My mind replays every scene. Every word spoken. I shiver, crossing my arms against my chest and rubbing my hands on my shoulders and upper arms. I tell myself it's because I'm cold, but I've never been a good liar.

The mountains are in front of me at a distance that makes them appear absolutely breathtaking. I can see the glaciers on the top and I know that if I were to hop into my car, I could be glacier sliding in two hours. I could be at my favorite cliff in an hour. Not that I'll go anywhere with tender bones, a setting sun, and no car.

What was I thinking? Why did I let him get so close? Why do I stay? It's not my home, and yet Adam has the answers. I know he does.

But I'm so exhausted. The small flashes of memory I've gotten are so different from the man I dream about. How can he be so completely different? He drinks too much, he swears even more, and he can go from laughing to yelling in the blink of an eye.

But his touch. One simple touch and I want to fall into his arms and never leave. One taste of him and I still haven't fully cooled off from the heat it sent through my body.

I take a deep breath, closing my eyes, and try to press it all to the back of my mind.

Feel me, Amy.

"Damn it!" I jump off the bench I'm sitting on and spin around, trying to find anything that looks familiar enough so I can figure out how to get home.

"Amy?" I turn back to the vaguely familiar voice.

Standing in front of me, hands in the pockets of his perfectly pressed khaki pants and dry-cleaned and starched light blue dress shirt, is Tyler. The boy who cheated on me. The boy who looks more like a man than he did the last time I saw him. "What are you doing here?" he asks.

I look around the empty park and wonder how he found me. There's a row of townhomes down the street and businesses line the other side.

I shrug. "I don't know where I am."

He takes another step forward, a friendly but cautious smile on his face. "Do you know who I am?"

I roll my eyes and sit back down, suddenly not in a hurry to go anywhere. "Yeah, Tyler. I know you." He lets out a slow breath and sits down next to me on the bench. It feels familiar, and even though Tyler cheated on me and I never talked to him after that, I'm not mad. Probably because I don't think I ever truly cared for him. His kisses certainly never left my head spinning.

"What are you doing here?"

He nods to a coffee shop on the corner. It doesn't look like anything special.

"I was walking to get a coffee. Want to join me?"

I frown and look around the neighborhood we're in. It's nice and safe. Middle-class, maybe. A little bit on the new side, I can't really tell. It's certainly nothing like the area where we grew up. "Do you live around here?"

He nods to a building that sits on top of a dry cleaner business. "Yeah, I live right there. I moved in right after graduation."

I look at the guy I dated for a year, the last guy I remember dating, and shake my head. Why does being with him feel okay, like nothing's changed, but every time I'm around Kelsey and Adam and my parents I feel like I'm one more strange comment away from snapping and going insane?

I take a seat in a leather chair in front of the fireplace while Tyler gets our coffees. I'm still rubbing my shoulders and my arms when he comes back. I give him an uncomfortable glance and watch him resting in the chair.

"So how'd you get lost tonight?" He peers at me over the edge of his paper cup, his lips puckered as he lightly blows to cool down his drink.

I do the same and then exhale. "I don't remember anything."

His eyebrows pull together. "You mean from tonight?"

"No. Since . . . well, you. I guess." I shrug like it's no big deal that I've lost two years of my life.

"Yeah, I heard about your accident. I'm glad you're okay, considering."

Yeah, I'm okay. I'm a bundled wreck that could snap at any second. I have dreams that terrify me, and I got lost taking a walk to cool down.

I stare off into the fire watching the yellow and red flames dancing in their cage. I can relate to the enclosed madness.

"So what happened to make you lost?"

I sigh and look at Tyler. I really take a good look at him. He's so handsome. I understand why my parents thought he was the perfect mate for me. Yes, my mother used that word. I swear she wanted a Labrador instead of a daughter. Lucky for her she got a nutcase.

"My boyfriend, Adam, and I got into a fight and I couldn't stay."

"Did he hurt you?" He leans forward and looks at me seriously. It almost makes me want to laugh. Oh, the irony.

"No, he didn't hurt me." I flash him an innocent smile. "You don't like him?"

With what I guess is a subconscious gesture, Tyler rubs the bridge of his now slightly crooked nose. "He broke my nose."

I raise an eyebrow. "You cheated on me."

"God, I was hoping you forgot that," he mutters, shaking his head and looking at the floor.

I gasp, mostly from shock, but then I see his horrified expression and I laugh. Loudly. If there were other customers in here right now, I'm sure we'd have the attention of everyone in the coffee shop.

"I'm so sorry," he starts to stutter out, his cheeks bright pink from embarrassment.

"Don't worry about it. I mean, other than being horribly inappropriate considering, it was the funniest and most honest thing I've heard."

I'm laughing so hard I have tears running down my cheeks, but I don't care. Tyler looks like he doesn't know what to do with me. Mental breakdown? Possibly. I have no idea either.

I'm trying to take a deep breath and regain some sense of control when I see a flash of purple and then I'm wrapped in someone's arm, or a chokehold, before I can blink.

My body freezes and I gasp, staring with wide eyes at Tyler over a mess of purple and hot pink. He shrugs, but his eyes are just as big as mine.

"Uh."

"Oh my gosh! Amy! You're back! I'm so excited to see you, but yeah . . . your accident. So I take it you're okay? Ready to come back? We've missed the ever lovin' shit out of you."

I recognize someone talking to me . . . quickly. So quickly I'm not sure she's stopping to breathe, but I can't say anything.

"Uh . . ." I try again, but the crook of her elbow is pressed against my throat, making speaking difficult.

She pulls back and I want to laugh. This—person—is pierced. Like, everywhere. I count at least four on her face and all I can see on her ears are flashes of silver and purple gauges in her lobes. The purple and pink I was smothered by is her hair. I've never seen anything, or anyone, quite like her.

And I know her?

Her face puckers up; her lips squishing together makes the piercing on her upper lip do a strange wiggle thing.

"Do I know you?" I finally choke out. Her hands are still on my shoulders, an odd look on her face, and then she looks at Tyler before looking slowly back at me.

"You don't remember?"

I shake my head. Remember what? Her? Uh, no. She's pretty unforgettable.

She bites her fingernail, which has a skull and crossbones painted on it. She's . . . odd. And then she looks at my dress and makes an expression on her face that probably mirrors mine.

"No, I'm sorry. I don't."

"Oh, shit. Adam said you'd come back to work when you remembered everything. I just assumed, since you're here."

"I work . . . here?" My eyes glance all over the coffee shop as she nods. It's far from a Starbucks. It's local, that's for sure. Artwork of the mountains is interspersed on the walls with posters for bands and open mic night at . . . Hooka Joe's?

I work at a place called Hooka Joe's. I snort.

"Yes, and you love it. We're like best friends. Well, except for Adam and Kelsey of course, but okay, we're like best coworker friends. Seriously."

My eyes get wider and wider with every high-pitched word she says. Best coworker friends? Those exist?

I look back at Tyler and he's choking on his drink. Or laughing. Whichever.

"Oh." Because really, what else do I say to her? "What's your name? I'm sorry, I don't mean to be rude, I just don't . . ."

"Remember." She cuts me off with a frown. It turns to a smile so quickly I wonder if it existed in the first place. "Adam told me everything. I'm Preston. We were all worried about you, but you're here!"

And with that final squeal, I'm wrapped in a death grip again, my hands frozen at my sides as she sort of lays half over the leather chair and almost in my lap. Squeezing me. Hard.

I cough and try to push her off and hear Tyler making some strange chortling sound in the background. I flip him off with my free hand.

"So anyway," she says as she pulls back again. "You don't remember yet. And gosh, that really forking sucks. But if you want your job back, we could use the help. Just let me know."

"Are you the manager?"

She stands to her full height, probably somewhere around five feet tall, and places her hands on her hips. "I'm the owner. You're the manager, at least during the daytime. I have Benjamin, who manages everything at night, but he's sick today."

My eyes go wider. I didn't even know they could grow this big. She's wearing a black skintight shirt with "Hooka Girl" in bright pink across the chest. It looks familiar, and then I remember where I've seen it. It's in my closet. I haven't worn it yet because I thought

Hooka was a band name, or short for Hooker. And that just seems like a weird thing to advertise across my breasts.

"So you'll call me, right?" Preston says as she walks away with a wide smile. "Get back on the schedule? No pressure, just whenever you're ready, let me know."

"Yeah . . ."

Tyler bows his head, and his entire body is shaking so hard I think he might be convulsing. I kick his shin.

"Shut up."

"Who in the hell was that?" he chokes out through his laughter.

I take the last sip of my drink, sorry that it's empty. She was kind of fun, even if a bit overwhelming. "Preston. My boss, I guess."

And then we both dissolve into another fit of laughter.

~

"Do you need a ride home?" Tyler asks me once he finishes his coffee and I sip on a fresh ice water. We've been talking for who knows how long, getting caught up. Apparently he bought a place in the neighborhood so he could finally live on his own before he goes to law school in the fall. I would have thought he'd be in some place nicer, but he said that his dad has insisted he learn to live like "one of the small people," so he gets a feel for what it's like to be an "average Joe" before he starts defending criminals. Yes. His dad said that to him. Our parents are peculiar people to say the least.

"Yeah, probably, since I don't know how to get there." I toss my water into the trash and grab my purse.

"Not a problem. What's your address?" he asks, pulling up a GPS app on his phone.

Well, shit. I have no idea.

"Umm. Hold on a second." I rush back inside and find Preston wiping down the glass dessert container. "Hey, Preston, do you know my address?"

Heat suffuses my cheeks and neck. This is so embarrassing. If she notices my mortification at having to ask the stupid question, she doesn't say anything.

She scribbles it down on a business card and hands it to me. "Want me to call Adam and have him come get you?" she asks as she glances at the door. Tyler is standing out there, proud as always with his hands in his front pockets, his back straight, and every article of clothing completely wrinkle-free. "Who's the stiff?"

I shake my head. "Just an old friend."

"No probs. Just call me with the number on the card whenever you want to come back." I thank her, and right as my hand is on the door, she calls my name. She has a wide grin on her face, not caring, or maybe not noticing, how strange this entire night has been for me. "I'm really glad you're back."

∼

I don't know anything right now. There's no way Adam can expect me to think straight when his lips are pressing against my neck, his hips are pressing me into the wall, and his hands are moving torturously slow up and down my arms. The bumps that are igniting all over my skin feel so hot that I think I might explode. I don't even remember how I got here. All I remember is Adam pulling Brendan off me in the parking lot and carrying me to Zander's car before throwing it into gear and driving full-throttle down the interstate until we pulled into the hotel.

Not a word has been spoken out loud but plenty has been said with our eyes.

I drop my head back against the wall and moan when his tongue darts out and licks against my collarbone, the soft spot of my flesh right behind it, and then up to my ear.

"Adam," I moan. I think. My hands grasp his hair and I don't know if I'm trying to pull him closer or push him away. My brain is fuzzy and my legs have turned to mush. There's too much emotion. Too much of everything in the room right now.

He pulls back and clasps his hands at the back of my neck, tilting me up so I can't look away.

He pierces me with a gaze so serious I think he could melt a block of ice. It's now that I remember what he asked me, what happened in the hallway at his fraternity's formal, and what I did shortly after.

How is it that he can turn me into such an emotional basket case? Will I always be this way around him? Crazy for him? Needing him so desperately that the thought of another woman's hands or lips on him can cause me to do the unthinkable? Because oh my shit—I kissed Brendan and told him to take me home. If going home with that dick-wad doesn't classify me as mentally insane, I'm not sure what would.

"You know I didn't kiss Britnee, right? You know that was her."

I close my eyes and see him in the hallway pressed up against her, his mouth on hers. "You kissed her back."

"It just took me a second to realize what she was doing. That's all, though. You know that, right? You have to know that."

Britnee's wicked smile flashes through my mind, and for the first time tonight, I'm able to breathe. "I know."

"Now tell me why you ran from the table in the first place. Tell me what freaked you out at the thought of making love to me tonight."

I hate it when Adam does this to me. He knows my secrets and my fears before even I know them sometimes. I don't understand how he can read me so well or put up with my constant indecision.

I shake my head, unable to tell him. To tell him that the thought of losing him makes me feel like I wouldn't survive. That I love him so much it hurts, physically. But at the same time, the thought of losing everything my family has ever given me is just as terrifying as losing him. They're both important to me and I never know which choice is the better one—not when he can't promise me forever.

He hasn't even defined what we have as a relationship, even though we've been having one for the last four months, and it's been the most amazing four months of my life.

His scruff scrapes my cheek and I shiver. I feel that movement all the way down to the tips of my toes as he brushes against me softly, and presses his hips—and his hardness—against me more firmly. "Tell me, Amy. I need to hear it."

I let out a low groan. Of frustration or need, I don't know. "You'll leave."

It's all I can gasp out before his lips are on mine again, his tongue pushing into my mouth and wrestling softly with mine. We move together like we've known each other our entire lives, and I can never understand how a touch or a kiss from this man can leave me feeling completely empty when he pulls away.

Which is exactly what he does, and I fall back against the wall. Every part of his body separates from mine and I'm left with nothing except the dark look in his eyes. His hands move to the wall next to my head. He's breathing heavily as he stares at me.

"You need to know two things right now, Amy Thompson." I blush at his use of my full name, but I can't take my eyes off him. His gaze is so heavy that I can still feel him pressing against me. "You are the only good thing that has ever happened to me in my life and I am not going anywhere. Ever."

I let that thought hit me, settle it into my bones, and try hard not to think about what it means. He can't be saying what I want him to. What I need him to.

He arches an eyebrow as if he's watched me process everything and is asking me if I'm done.

"And the other?" I ask, although I'm not sure I want to know. I'm still caught on the "ever" word of his last thought.

"I never knew it would be possible for a fuckup like me to fall in love, but I did. And now that I feel it, I really . . . really want to show you how much I love you."

With a wicked grin, he doesn't give me time to think about what he just said. Because holy crap, I don't know if I'd believe him if I had to think about it without his hands moving on me. Because they are. His hands are back on my body with a ferociousness that I have never experienced before in my life. I can barely catch my breath while we claw at each other like animals.

This is what I needed to hear. It's what I needed to know, and now that I've heard it, I'm taking everything I can from this man. I'm giving him everything I have because he's the only one I've ever met worth giving it to. Not just sex—but my entire heart, body, and soul. I no longer want to exist in my carefully planned life. I want to be the one driving my decisions and my life. And I want to do both with him.

Our clothes are shed before I can take a breath. I don't even know how it happened. Did Adam take them all off? Did I help? My head is filled with a powerful lust and love combination, and only the feel of Adam pressing both of my hands against the wall above my head brings me fully back to the present.

"Adam," I moan as I arch my hips into his. I can feel his erection run across my thighs and all I want is him in me. I need him. I need to feel every part of him, just like he needs to know that I have no doubts about him. Not after what he just said.

His forehead presses against mine. I can feel a slight layer of sweat against his skin, and I look at him, wanting to see him. His eyes are tightly closed as if he's trying to stay in control.

Who cares about control? I lost mine the minute Adam's lips touched mine the first time months ago.

"I need you to be sure, Amy." His forehead rubs against mine. I'm thrown between the forcefulness of his grip on my hands and the soft-ness in his voice and his words.

I close my eyes and do what Adam tells me to always do when I start getting stressed about the future. Just feel it. Feel us.

And it works just like always. We may not make any sort of sense on paper, but when I let the bullshit and the worries go, we always feel right. Like now.

I nod my head against his and smile. "I'm sure."

"Thank fuck," he growls with a hoarse voice, and then his lips are back on mine. His hand is on my waist, moving lower and then lifting my thigh so it's raised and wrapped around his hip. "Legs around me, now."

I listen to him, moving before he's even finished speaking. I almost feel like an animal rutting in the wild, but I can't help it. And I wouldn't stop it even if I could.

The tip of his erection presses against me and his hand on my hip lowers me onto him. And then he pulls me closer, filling me more com-pletely and powerfully than I would have thought possible.

"I love you," I moan as soon as he begins to rock against me. He presses me against the wall and down onto him at the same time. I repeat the words, kissing him all over, groaning the words into his neck and against any part of his skin that I can reach with my lips and my tongue. I relish the feel of his hands gripping my waist and my hands with an equal amount of pressure, as his lips press against my neck, returning the three words with the same amount of passion that I give to him.

"Amy . . ."

"Oh my . . ." I feel myself hit the top of the roller coaster. My insides squeeze him farther into me, and I know that any second the roller coaster is going to drop and it's going to be the most exquisite and powerful moment of my life.

"Amy . . ."

He rocks me against the wall harder, and then opens his eyes as I shatter into a thousand pieces as he calls my name again.

EIGHT

Amy."

I can't stop from trembling at the sound of my name, the way he feels inside me and pressing against me. His hands feel like molten lava all over my skin, melting me and taking away every worry I've ever had. Every thought.

"Amy." The word and the name is the same, but the tone is different than it was a second ago. It's clearer, but softer, and . . . oh no . . .

"Amy."

Oh my God.

"Wake up, Amy. Tell me you're okay."

My eyes snap open and I'm looking directly into Adam's eyes. His hand is on my shoulder, warming my already sweating skin, and there's a frown line deeply ingrained in between his eyes.

In a split second, I'm curled into the far corner of my bed. Skittering away from him with my knees tucked up to my chest and my arms wrapped around my knees. I don't take my eyes off Adam as he stands up, frowning at me and my completely insane reaction to him.

"Another dream?" he asks drily, and then he turns to leave with his shoulders slightly hunched forward.

I open and close my mouth half a dozen times before he reaches my door to say something—anything—that will end his pain, but nothing comes. All I can think about is the way he felt when he screwed me against the wall at the Lux Hotel, just as he told me about yesterday.

And now, all I'm looking at are the muscles on his back, the back of his arms, and his legs that are so perfectly defined that, for a split second, I think I might still be dreaming.

"Wait!" I think I sound panicky, as if the thought of him walking out the door could be the worst thing in the world. Awake, it doesn't make any sense, but as I recall the now blurring images of my dream, this is how I would feel. I know it. The thought of Adam walking out the door and away from me, not understanding what I just saw, would gut me.

At least the me who I was in my dream.

And this morning, regardless of the arguing we did yesterday, I don't want him walking out the door.

Adam is facing me with a resigned expression. As if he knows the next words out of my mouth will once again hurt him, even if I don't mean to. "What is it?"

How do I explain to him how confused I feel? I blink, wanting to answer him, but then I see him. Truly see him for the first time. He's even better looking than he was in my dream. His chest is rippled and defined. He has a tattoo in scrolling print that's written sideways down the ribs on his right side, and he's only wearing a pair of boxer briefs. Tightly fitted boxer briefs.

I swallow, my cheeks heating, and turn from him, suddenly nervous as the images of my dream replay through my mind. With my fingers, I pick at the comforter that used to be mine in the apartment I shared with Kelsey.

"Amy?" I don't have to look up to know he's walking back toward me. I can hear the soft padding of his feet against the carpet. I can feel him coming closer, cautiously.

Not even sure what I'm doing, my slightly trembling hand presses into the side of the bed. My voice is just as shaky as my hand. "Sit with me?"

It comes out as a question even though that wasn't my intention. Why do I want him in my bed? I don't. He scares me. I should be getting out of my bed, not inviting him into it. Although this morning, with my head groggy and un-caffeinated, I wonder if Adam does scare me—has always scared me—but maybe for a different reason than the one I've been thinking.

He sits down at the opposite corner of the bed. I can't seem to bring my eyes up from the tattered edges of the comforter as I feel the bed shift under his weight. I wonder what I would see in his eyes if I were brave enough to look at him.

I gather my courage and look, and then laugh, because he's sitting with one leg tucked under him on the bed and the other foot tapping nervously against the floor. He's looking everywhere in the room except at me.

Adam's head snaps to mine and I meet his gaze dead-on. With what I assume is a nervous gesture, he bites one side of his bottom lip and cocks his head to the left.

"I don't bite," I tell him, shifting so there's room for both of us.

He releases a small sigh and, this time, I know it's not out of frustration. It's contentment, and I can see it written all over his face as his body climbs into the bed next to me and the stress around his eyes disappears.

Heat hits my cheeks when I realize what I've just done, and my fingers tighten along the edges of the sheets. Adam's arms are crossed against his bare chest and his legs are stretched out, crossed at the ankles. There is not an ounce of fat on this man. Not a single inch of this man has anything on it that doesn't belong. I let my eyes drift down his legs, trying to remember how they felt when they spread my knees and carried the weight of my body as he pressed me against the wall.

He's just so . . . strong. If possible, my dream didn't do him justice.

"So do you wanna talk about it?" he finally asks. The question breaks the heavy silence and my perusal of his body. His head is resting against my headboard, his eyes lightly closed. If what I felt in the dream is true, then Adam hasn't missed a single second of the way I've just admired his body. He's simply let me have it.

I mirror his look, with my head resting on the headboard, and face him. The edges of the wooden board press against the space behind my ear, slightly uncomfortably, but I don't move.

"Nope." But my breath hitches on the word. I know he caught it when his lips fight against a smile. A knowing grin.

He turns to face me with a curious look and I focus not on his eyes that still seem able to read me, but on the way his hair falls back against his forehead and his unshaven cheeks and chin. It all looks a bit messy and wild and somehow seems so perfectly him.

He raises an eyebrow, and I can see the humor in his eyes. "But it wasn't bad?"

I laugh softly, refusing to take my eyes from his, because in this moment—whatever it is that's going on—I want him to know. That I'm sorry I don't remember. I'm sorry I can't feel everything the way he wants me to, but hell if I don't want to try as hard as I possibly can to be the girl who feels him.

Without taking my eyes off him, I move my left hand closer to him until it's resting on his thigh. We're barely touching and there's no pressure on my hand to press down into him, but his muscles tense and something flares in his eyes.

"No. It wasn't bad."

His thigh tenses under my hand and then relaxes when I don't remove it from his skin. My pinky is just barely touching the edges of his boxer briefs and the soft cotton is a different texture from the roughness of his hard skin mixed with his prickly hair. But yet together, they both feel perfect against my soft skin.

Slowly, as if he's afraid I'll bolt or kick him out of my bed, he smiles at me and his hand covers mine on his thigh. He presses down firmly on the back of my skin so my fingers dig into his leg a little bit. The warmth and change in pressure sends shock waves up my arm and into my chest. I close my eyes, afraid of what he'll see in them if I keep them open.

"Good." I can't tell if he's smiling or not, but his tone sounds serious. And deeper—more gravelly—than before.

Willing myself to be brave, to take this moment in and just let it be, I open my eyes and watch his hand move against mine. His fingers press against my hand, massaging it softly, and then they slide into the space between my fingers.

The tips of his fingers lightly rub against my skin, all the way down to the tips of my fingers, and my breath hitches just watching the way his fingers can move against me.

Some of my dreams make me question whether they're real or not. If they're memories or fantasies. But with the way his slight touch lights up my skin and my nerves like the Fourth of July fireworks, one thing is certain.

That dream was real. One hundred percent.

～

"I'm sorry about yesterday." His voice cuts through the silence we've been sharing while we eat our breakfast. I haven't been able to say a word to him since he climbed out of bed, held out his hand, and pulled me to the kitchen where he sat me down and began making me French toast.

"I didn't mean to push you. I just miss you." I nod once and offer him the briefest smile. "And I love you, so much. Just give this some time, okay? It's only been a month since you woke up. Everything will be okay soon."

"What happens if it's not? What happens if once I remember everything, I decide this isn't where I want to be?"

He drizzles unnecessary amounts of syrup over this breakfast. When he's done, he wipes a few drips off the bottle and licks it off his thumb with his tongue.

"You will." It's spoken with a quiet confidence, but with such an underlying darkness that I have to fight the urge to squirm in my chair.

I choke down my bile and close my eyes, refocusing on the part of yesterday that upset me more than the way I felt when his hands and lips were all over me.

"I met Preston last night." His head snaps up and he looks at me with wide eyes. I take a deep breath, willing myself to calm down. I don't want to fight with him again. Not today. Not this morning when I feel like maybe we've taken three steps forward instead of our occasional one. "Why didn't you tell me when I asked if I had a job?"

I asked Adam weeks ago, while I was still in the hospital, if I had a job to get back to. All he told me was "no." Adam's head drops down and I can see his deep exhale through the movement in his shoulders.

"I should have been told." My voice is firm, not angry, but filled with hurt. "How am I supposed to remember anything when no one tells me the truth?"

I don't wait for his answer as I clear our empty plates and rinse them off in the sink.

"I'm sorry." He stands from the chair and takes a step forward before stopping. My spine prickles. Not because I'm afraid of him hurting me, but because I'm in the same place I found myself yesterday before he pushed me up against the wall.

I walk around him, out of the kitchen, and into the living room while he starts talking, defending his actions.

"I know you're mad, and you have every right to be. We—Kelsey and I—didn't want to push you. Your neurologist told us you'd remember things on your own but that putting too much pressure on you, or throwing too much at you, could make it take longer." He puffs out his cheeks, resting his hands against the back of the chair that sits opposite me in the living room, and blows out a breath. "I just . . . you have to understand, Amy. When you woke up, you had no idea about anything in your life."

He shakes his head. I can see his pain. I can feel it radiating from across the room, but I hope he equally feels how upset I am. How am I supposed to remember anything when no one *tells* me anything?

"I thought it'd be easier, Kelsey and I both did, to listen to the doctors and let you remember everything gradually. Hell, Amy, I was going to let you move back home to be with your parents even though I *know* it's the last place you'd ever want to be again."

"Then why am I here?"

"Because your mom thought it'd be best for you to go back to your real life."

"So my real life is slinging coffee at Hooka Joe's in some dumpy part of town, and I live in a dump with a boyfriend that lies to me. I gotta tell ya, it doesn't seem like much of a life we have right now."

I see the pain slice right through him as he flinches at my words. I regret them instantly. Something feels wrong as I sit on the couch acting like a coldhearted bitch, directing all my anger and frustration at him.

"I'm not trying to be a bitch, Adam." I sigh, falling back into the chair, and press the heels of my palms into my eyes.

"Listen," he finally says, "I'm trying to do what's best for you, and I'm sorry I screwed up. I'm sorry, truly, that I didn't tell you about your job. I *want* you to remember. I want you to remember why you love this little dump; which you chose, by the way."

One side of my nose twitches as I take in the tiny apartment. It's not a dump, not really. Just small.

"Yes, you chose this place. And someday you'll know why, but I don't want to force you into anything. I just want you to come back to me."

"What if I don't?"

"You will." Those two words are filled with the same confidence from earlier but this time it's matched by his heated stare. It pins me to the couch, not allowing me to look away.

"You sound so sure."

He shrugs, not one of nonchalance, but confidence. It almost makes me smile. Almost. "I've seen our story. I've lived it, and I know how it ends."

I take the bait. I can't help it. I need to know. I need to know why it is that he scares the hell out of me—awake and now in my dreams, and yet, I can't just pack up and walk away. Go start a life that's one of my own making instead of stories I don't understand. "How's that?"

"Together."

I wrinkle my nose, but I can't argue; mostly because I still don't know if he's right or not.

"You said something in my dream about not working at my dad's firm."

He licks his lips and then presses them together. I know the move by now. He's stalling or debating how much truth to give me. "Your dad lined up a job for you when you graduated, at his old tax firm, and you turned it down."

"Why, though?" That had always been the plan. I was always supposed to go to college, major in finance, and work where my dad did. That plan was set in stone before I ever stepped foot into high school. Turning it down is not only surprising, but I bet my parents flipped their shit.

He raises one eyebrow and leans forward, resting his elbows on his knees, and watches me intently. "Do you really see yourself working at a tax firm, stuck in a cubicle farm, every day for the rest of your life?" He pauses, waiting for my reaction. As soon as I open my mouth to answer, he stops me. "Don't answer based on the plan, Amy. Think about it. Think about who you are and what you've always wanted for yourself, even before I came into the picture."

I breathe out a puff of air, frustrated that he can't just answer the question for once. Then I close my eyes and rest my head on the back of my chair. I want to tell him, "Yes, of course I wanted that," but as I open my mouth to speak the words, I can't. Even as I think the words, something doesn't feel right about them.

The thought of working in that office makes me feel as uncomfortable as the dresses and shoes I bought that look like they belong to me but don't fit the way I want them to.

And I know, without even having to answer him, that he's right. Something has changed within me. Somehow I broke away from the life my parents predetermined I should live.

"That's why my parents drained my bank account," I finally say, quietly. Adam doesn't say anything. He doesn't have to. Without opening my eyes, I can feel him smiling at me from across the room. "And that's why I work at Hooka Joe's. I couldn't afford the apartment anymore."

When I finally do open my eyes, startled by this revelation but somehow unsurprised by it at the same time, Adam shrugs his shoulders.

"You wanted to be free."

I want to open my mouth to say something, but I can't. The memory of sitting at Martino's and crying on Adam's shoulder while I watched the butterflies dance from the ceiling flashes through my mind.

Now I know why I was so upset that day.

NINE

I don't always understand how I know things I do without having an actual memory attached to them, but every once in a while it happens. Or it's beginning to.

Yesterday, when I walked into the kitchen, I stared at the black-and-white photo mural on our wall and knew—just knew—that I was the one who created that gorgeous masterpiece. I don't remember the hours I must have spent finding the perfect photos, editing them so they were all black and white, finding the perfect frames, or spray-painting others black. But that's what I did.

It must have taken me days, if not weeks, to complete the project and hang it all so perfectly on the wall that you can't help but get lost in the smiles and the memories that I've preserved.

A labor of love. And it's mine.

And before last week, I also couldn't tell you the difference between a latte, macchiato, and cappuccino, except for maybe the flavoring if it was required. But when I showed up to work the other day, after calling Preston to see if I could come back, it only took minutes of training for me to know how to do everything.

It's like it's instinct, so deeply ingrained in me I could prepare the perfect coffee drink in my sleep. And there's been something oddly thrilling, if not comforting, in the fact that for the first time in a month, there's finally a place that I fit.

Even if it is just knowing how to make a medium skinny soy caramel mocha, iced with an extra shot of whipped cream, to perfection.

"This isn't the drink I pegged you for," I say with a genuine smile, and slide the cup across the counter to the customer.

He flashes me a smile and tucks his wallet into the back of his perfectly pressed pants.

"What can I say, Amy? I'm a new man." Tyler looks around the small coffee bar and takes his first sip of his drink. "Do you have a break coming up?"

"I don't think Preston will mind. I'm not on the clock today anyway."

I wave him away to get a seat while I mix myself almost the same drink I made for Tyler. Except mine is full fat with dairy not soy because that's just gross. I figure if you're going to consume four hundred and fifty calories in a drink, you might as well make them count.

"What are you doing here?" I ask once we're sitting in a corner table near a small stage that has a few stools and two microphones for open mic night. It's nothing special, but I can see how customers could enjoy coming here to listen to music as they relax on some of the overused microfiber sofas and oversized plaid chairs. None of the furniture matches, yet it all fits.

But it doesn't seem like a place Tyler would spend much time in, if any at all.

His sheepish grin tells me he's busted. "I saw your car out front, so I thought I'd stop in and say hi. See how the other night went when you got home." He says this last part with a quiet and concerned voice. It's laced with suspicion, as if he wants to check out my arms hidden under my sleeves and look for bruises.

"I figured today was as good as any to get back to my life." I shrug and take a sip of my drink, allowing the coolness of the creamy iced coffee to bring me a second's pleasure. I think that Tyler's concern is going overboard. The problem is that I don't blame him. Adam did break his nose, and I'm not always entirely sure how stable he is either.

But hurt me? Physically? I'm not sure Adam is capable of that by any means. Emotionally? That's a whole different ball game. The things I've seen, the memories I've had—even if they were slight glimpses—make me feel like the beginning of our relationship was some big game to him. Or me, maybe. But it must have calmed down at some point and become real, right? Because if not, what are we still doing together?

The only thing I can't deny is the way my body reacts to his, even if I wish it didn't.

I shake the thoughts and questions out of my head. The answers exist; except just like always, they're out of my reach.

"Adam was fine. Worried, but fine." He doesn't look like he believes it fully, but he shrugs. We finish our drinks talking about his boring day as an intern at some small law firm downtown. And when Preston isn't looking, we laugh about the hassle it must be for her to fly with all that metal she has to remove during security.

Not maliciously, though. And Preston seems used to people gawking and giggling about her. I was surprised at how quickly she welcomed me back into the coffee shop. She spent the first morning talking nonstop. Literally. I'm not sure if she's simply overly caffeinated from owning the coffee bar, or if it's her natural personality, but the girl can talk. And talk. Without breathing. It's the most strangely fascinating thing I've ever seen.

She looks like some badass punk or goth chick with her piercings, wicked dye job, and skintight black clothing. She's almost intimidating, even if she's the size of a puppy. But then she talks and sounds as if she believes fairy tales are the spice of life. It's a strange combination but equally endearing.

The best part is that she talks to me like she's seen me every day for the last three months, which is apparently how long I've worked at Hooka Joe's. She doesn't give me the pitiful look I'm used to seeing. She doesn't tiptoe around me like I could crumble to my knees at any second. And most importantly, she doesn't keep asking, "Do you remember this?" like so many people, including Adam and Kelsey, have a tendency to do.

She's completely refreshing.

When our drinks are done, I tell Preston that I'm going to walk Tyler outside. There are only a few customers anyway, so she waves me away like she's been doing all day. I can't decide if she simply trusts me or if she's this laid back with all of her employees.

"Thanks for stopping to check on me," I tell him once we're outside.

"Not a problem. I just want you to know that I'm here if you need anything. I don't know what you're going through, but if you need an ear, or a friend . . ." His voice trails off as his gaze catches something behind me. His friendly smile tightens right before he leans in and brushes his lips against my cheek. I flinch away from him, but if he notices, he doesn't say anything. "I'll see you soon."

And then he turns and walks away, leaving me watching him with a confused look.

"How long have you been seeing him?"

I jump at the cold voice coming from behind me. Each word punctuated precisely, as if he's not trying to spit something out of his mouth.

My eyes widen and my back straightens as I slowly turn to face Adam. His hands are shoved deeply into his dark blue jeans. He exhales a breath, and it takes one second for his teeth to grind together. Amazing how I don't know this man but can read him so well.

I look back to the spot Tyler just walked away from, but he's gone.

I frown. "I'm not seeing him. He showed up here the other night when I was lost in the park and then today he came in for a drink when he saw my car." I look around the park across the street and scan for the dry cleaners. "He lives over in that building," I tell him, pointing to the apartment Tyler told me he lived in.

His lips twist into a funny shape, like he's trying to hold back saying something he might regret. "But you like being with him." It's a statement not a question, and I understand his implication. I like being with Tyler and not him.

I look away, not knowing what to say. I can't even deny it. Tyler and I have a history that isn't complicated by me not remembering things. By the time I lost my memory, Tyler wasn't really in my life anymore, so anything that happened in the last two years is as much of a mystery to him as it is to me.

"Being with him doesn't come with pressure to feel anything." My words are soft and not meant to hurt, but I can tell they do. It's not my intent, but I can't make him feel better about me being around someone either. It's completely innocent. "You have to remember that I grew up with him. I know him."

He opens his mouth to say something but quickly closes it, fidgeting back and forth on his heels, flexing his fingers. He's angry and I want to explain to him that it's no big deal, but I can't find the words. I'm not sure I have anything to be sorry for besides talking to a friend over a coffee and slacking at my job.

He blinks slowly. "I stopped by to see if you want to go get some dinner."

"I told Kelsey I'd have dinner with her at the bar." I rock back and forth on my feet, nervous under Adam's searing gaze. I watch his anger at seeing me with Tyler slowly disappear, and a sparkle appears in his eyes.

"Great. I'll go with you."

I stare at him for a second before nodding. I don't know what to say or why he wants to be with me so badly, but I'll let him just so I don't have to hear his teeth grind together anymore when he's mad at me.

∾

The Library is the biggest hole-in-the-wall, dirty bar I have ever seen in my entire life, or at least remember seeing. I hate that I qualify every statement with that these days.

I blow out a heavy breath as soon as I enter. The bar is narrow. Two pool tables in the far back, one row of booths to the left, and the bar on the right. It's just a few blocks off campus, and the name makes me laugh. How many college kids say they're going to the library but don't mean the one with actual books? Did *I* talk about going to The Library in this way?

"Thank God you're finally here," Kelsey says with a huge smile, and wraps her arms around me. "These stupid college kids here for the summer have been driving me insane all night."

I roll my eyes and slide into the booth. "Didn't we, like, just graduate? They're not any different, are they?"

Kelsey waves her hand dismissively. "These are the kids who have nothing better to do than get wasted all day and all night. Trust me," she says while pointing to three couples at the end of the bar. The girls are wearing what looks like matching dresses, and the guys all have khaki shorts, flips-flops, and button-down shirts with the sleeves rolled up. Good God, did they all plan their outfits?

"They've been here since noon. Seven hours of nonstop drinking, and if those girls don't get out of here soon, I'm liable to kick 'em out just because they're blonde and stupid."

I look at Kelsey, but her eyes are narrowed in their direction. Except the girls aren't paying attention to their drinks or their dates anymore. They're leaning so far over in order to get Zander's attention that their boobs are hanging on the bar.

I blink and think I might actually see a hint of nipple.

These girls . . . they seem so familiar. The realization hits me and I gasp and look at Kelsey. Those girls are me. Or at least who I tried to go back to being the other week with the preppy little dresses and designer sandals. And the boys? They're walking mirror images of Tyler.

The girls giggle and flip their hair, and I'm reminded of the first frat party Kelsey and I went to our freshman year. We thought just because we were rich, dressed right, and knew we were at least halfway decent looking, we could have anything—anyone—we wanted.

These girls have the same energy to them. And I despise them. Something inside me wants to walk up to them and shake them. Shake the sense into them that they're better than this, they're better than the act, and to grow the fuck up.

Except what kind of hypocrite does that make me?

"This is some place," I say, looking around the small area and turning away from the trio of perfection at the bar. I can't handle the way it makes me feel to see them. To know I used to be them but not know how I freed myself from the lure of wealth and entitlement. "How did Zander end up owning it?"

"His grandpa used to own it, but he died a few months back."

While she's talking, she doesn't take her eyes off Zander. He's almost as good-looking as Adam, but in an even rougher way.

Where Adam looks like an Abercrombie model that stepped into darkness or messed around in it for a while, Zander looks like he's lived the darkness and barely broken through the other side. His left arm has a full sleeve of tattoos, one side of his top lip has a small piercing, and his black hair is cropped short. He looks part military, part badass, with a hint of rockstar in him.

And he's with Kelsey. My beautiful friend who doesn't—or didn't—trust anyone not to hurt her, is currently looking at him like he just reached up and hung the moon in the sky just for her.

"He doesn't seem like the bartending type." He looks too rough to tend bar. More like he'd fit in better in the back booth swinging back shots of Jack Daniel's and willing to kick anyone's ass who tried to get him to move.

"He's not," Kelsey says softly, admirably. "But his loyalty to his grandpa runs deep, and there was no way he'd give this place up to anyone else."

I feel like we're all sitting around our table, mesmerized by the rough-looking guy behind the bar. He's such a contradiction. His tattoos and piercing give him a rough shape that says he can handle his own, the smile for the ladies says he can take care of them if they ask nice enough, but the coldness in his eyes—the look that doesn't change when he smiles or growls—says maybe he's just a little bit lost himself.

"What about his parents?" I ask, taking a sip of my rum and coke.

The only indication Adam heard me over the music blaring from the speakers is a slight twitch by his nose. "They're worthless fuckers. Worse than mine."

He doesn't take his eyes off Zander as he throws his bottle of beer back and then sets it down on the table harder than necessary.

"He doesn't talk about them." Kelsey's voice is as soft as I've ever heard it. She's not a soft and loving person by nature. I think the only other time I've heard her sound like this is when I first woke up from my coma.

But as I look at her, she smiles at me sadly and shrugs. "I figure it's not worth fighting over. Someday if he's ready, he'll let me know what happened."

"You don't want to know, Kels." Adam looks at her with a warning in his eyes that I imagine is trying to intimidate her, but it doesn't bother her in the least.

"So you've said," she snaps rudely.

"I don't understand," I say, looking back and forth between the two of them. I can't understand why Adam feels the need to protect Zander—who looks completely capable of taking care of himself—against Kelsey of all people.

"Zander's had a tough life, Amy. And one he doesn't talk about. Can we just leave it at that?" By the way Adam's eyes are narrowed toward me and the edge his voice takes on, I take it as the rhetorical question it's intended to be.

"I can't believe your parents don't care that you live above a bar." I smile, and Kelsey snickers. And this isn't the five-star dining kind of bar or lounge that would be suitable to the standards of Kelsey's parents, her dad in particular. This place is maybe a half star.

She shrugs. "My dad likes that Zander doesn't give a shit about football, and they're not like your parents. They just want me to be happy."

"Where mine . . ." I begin, but she cuts me off with a smile.

"Want you to do what makes them happy."

My lips wrap around the straw of my drink, and I take a long sip, thinking about it. It doesn't take me long to figure out she's completely right. And slowly, the bar doesn't seem so small and dumpy. It feels a bit more like a home. And the coffee bar, where I've been struggling with how I ended up slinging drinks for a living, doesn't seem like a step down. Every day I've been there it's begun to feel more like I'm around family.

I ignore the questions I have about Adam, I push aside my lack of memories, and I realize that my life, while it's different from what I remembered it being, isn't so bad after all.

⁓

Things are changing. Slowly moving at the pace of a snail, and some days it's incredibly frustrating. When I'm left alone to the quiet of my apartment for too long, I want to have all my memories back, neatly in place exactly where they belong. I want the puzzle completed instead of having to slowly piece it back together bit by bit, not sure if I'm putting the pieces in the right place until the next memory comes along.

Unfortunately, it's not happening as quickly as I'd like it to.

But things are getting better.

Preston is incredible to be around, and I'm back to working full-time at the coffee shop. Zander came in the other night and played a set during open mic night. His voice was amazing. Rich and dark and it lured in all the women, but he didn't notice a single person in the room besides Kelsey. He sang directly to her for the entire hour he was on the small stage with his acoustic guitar.

I served coffee, iced drinks, and smoothies the entire night with a smile on my face. It isn't a place I ever would have felt like I belonged, and yet somehow, I fit here.

The customers know me, even if I don't remember them, and yet they're not the type of crowd to care. Almost everyone who comes into Hooka's looks either stoned or like a tortured artist. Or both.

They don't ask me questions that I don't know how to answer.

Adam sat on a wobbly stool the entire night with a smile on his face and a drink in his hand, watching me work and making jokes while I refilled orders.

And sometimes Tyler comes in and we sit and talk.

It's platonic, completely, and yet I don't mention it to Adam because I don't want to start another fight. But it helps to have Tyler to talk to. We can talk about our childhoods and laugh at our parents, and the more I do it, the more I take the time to remember how I was raised and how I grew up, the more the tiny mismatched apartment doesn't seem nearly as bad.

It's beginning to feel more like home every day.

"We're here."

I turn to Adam and smile. We're both dressed in running shorts and tank tops, and the early summer weather in Colorado is finally nice enough to do some hiking. Which is what I insisted on today. Although, as I look at the entrance to the state park, I frown.

"I thought we were going to the cliffs."

Adam shakes his head and opens the door to his car. "This place is better."

"No place is better than the cliffs," I argue halfheartedly, but I'm already climbing out of the car and waiting for Adam to grab the backpack full of food.

"Just wait," he says, and holds out his hand. I take it easily because it's becoming easier to be around him.

It doesn't help me understand much of who I am anymore, but slowly I'm beginning to think that it may not matter how I became this girl. Because admittedly, being with Adam and enjoying my job at Hooka's is a lot less stressful than I ever remember my life before being.

We walk the slow-climbing hiking path, holding hands, but speaking very little. It's the first hike I've been on since my casts came off, and I'm content to enjoy the walk, the weather, and the company in silence.

The weather is perfect, there isn't a cloud in the sky, and we follow a path that dances around a small creek where small bright yellow flowers grow along the edges. This is everything I love about Colorado.

Some people love the snow-skiing, which can't be beat, or the city with its never-ending list of concerts and nightlife and sporting events. But give me a creek filled with cold mountain water, a bright blue sky, and the fresh air that always seems to have a slightly chilled bite as you breathe it in, and I'm in heaven.

"Oh my . . ." My voice trails off as Adam leads me off the path and stops at the top of a small mountain crest. We're far below the tree line, but I'm wide-eyed in amazement at the small area of rocky hot springs below us.

A light mist or fog escapes from the water and drifts upward, evaporating into the chilly air. The water is so calm it reflects the bright blue sky, making the water seem as blue as a pool in someone's backyard.

It's magnificent.

"Cool, right?" Adam says, and tugs my hand down onto the blanket he removed from his backpack. I snort at his word choice. This is beyond cool. This is incredible, breathtaking, and heaven all wrapped up in a private party of two.

"How did you find this place?"

I can't seem to pull my eyes off the rocks and the water below us to the man next to me. My voice sounds dazed. I *feel* dazed.

"We found it last summer. Zander and Kelsey like to come here."

I make a face and reluctantly pull my eyes to his. His knees are bent and his arms are wrapped around them, one hand lightly holding on to the wrist of his other arm.

He doesn't watch me take him in, but I do, and I see all of him. His slightly crooked nose, deep-set honey-colored eyes that have the ability to light up like the sun and turn as dark as mud, striking cheekbones, and his unshaved scruff that I long to run a fingernail across to see if the brief memories I've had of him kissing me are true.

Will I still feel him on my skin even when he isn't there?

I linger on him, breathing him in, and revel in the fact that I know he's letting me look. I can see his pulse thumping at the bottom of his neck as he stretches it to the left and right, popping it before he stays still again, and bites the inside of his bottom lip.

I can't help the thoughts anymore, and I've long since given up on trying to.

I stare at the pictures in our apartment, and when I close my eyes at night, I try to remember how he looked in my dreams when he pushed me against a wall and made love to me. Kelsey called him sex on a stick.

I simply think he's sexy in a dangerous sort of way.

We haven't done anything except hold hands since that day he kissed me in the kitchen, but at night when we say good-night, I see the lust and war in his eyes as he debates whether or not to lean in and brush his lips against mine.

Some nights I duck into my room quickly just so I don't see the look of disappointment in his eyes when I turn my head away a second too soon.

I shake my head, clearing my lustful and ridiculous thoughts.

"How often did we come here?" I ask, my voice sounding a little bit dry.

Adam turns to me slowly, a lazy grin on his face when he sees my cheeks flushing from the heat of checking him out.

"With them or alone?"

His voice pours over me like chocolate fudge. Thick and dripping with innuendo that I can't ignore.

I look back to the public springs and back to him.

"You're kidding." We did not have sex here. There's no way I would do something so risqué, so completely open to the public where anyone could walk by and see. "Aren't you?"

He raises and lowers one shoulder and raises his eyebrows. "What do you think?"

I stare at the water as if it holds the answers. There's no way.

"I wouldn't do that," I say quietly, doubtfully.

But I can feel something unfurling in my belly like an animal slowly waking from a season of hibernation. I feel the heat rise from my chest up to my cheeks, and at the same time, even my fingertips feel like they've touched a fire's flame.

"Would I?" I ask with wide eyes.

Adam simply smiles and shrugs. "Would you? Ice Princess Amy may not have," he says, and gives me a challenging grin—a knowing grin—and the heat in my stomach increases. I watch a memory dance across his eyes as if he's lost in ecstasy. From what he's implying, he may be. "But would *you*?"

I feel the implication pressing against me down to the tips of my toes. The Amy I was before him is gone, and in its place isn't a new Amy, just me. The girl I am with him. I stare at the water, boring my eyes into the misty fog as if willing an answer to appear out of the air. It doesn't, but by the way Adam is smiling at me, I already know the answer.

We had sex here. We made love in this very place. I choke softly on the thought and Adam laughs once, a deep-sounding husky laugh when he realizes I've come to the right conclusion even if I don't have the memory.

This is wild and it's not me, but it is. This is something the girl who goes to rock concerts and works at Hooka's and lives in an apartment with mismatched furniture would totally do.

I can almost see myself freely taking off my clothes and jumping into the water just to seduce the man next to me. I can see it as though it's happening in front of me. I can feel Adam's hands on my hips, while I straddle his lap and rock against him, pushing him into the rounded edges of the rocks. I hold on to him for balance and bite his shoulder to keep from crying out too loudly and risk being heard or seen.

I shake my head back and forth, but the thoughts don't clear.

If it's not a memory, what is it? A fantasy? Something I want to do with him, or something I've already done?

"Are you ready for lunch?" he asks with humor in his voice. It takes me another second to blink back my visions.

I turn to him, almost afraid of what he'll see in my face, scared that desire and lust will be so blatantly tattooed onto my skin.

When he catches my eye, he simply smirks and hands me a sandwich.

TEN

I want to go in," I stand up and brush the crumbs from my eaten sandwich off my lap.

Adam raises one eyebrow. "In your clothes?"

I shrug, and look from the water back to him. "Why not?"

He looks to the rocks with an expression I don't understand on his face, but he's not happy about me wanting to go down there.

"I don't think we should," he says, but his voice sounds far away.

"Then stay here, but there's no way I can't go test the water."

I don't understand the sudden hesitation, when just twenty minutes ago he was teasing me about sex in the hot water. It's obvious we've been in before, and the trek down isn't long or dangerous looking.

He huffs out a frustrated breath and uncurls his body from the ground, standing next to me after kicking off his shoes.

"Lead the way."

I take a step back from Adam's outstretched hand and kick off my shoes. Then I cross my arms in front of me and grab the bottom of my tank top, grinning while Adam's eyes widen slightly and his cheeks pale.

I quickly remove my shirt and stand in front of him with nothing on but my yoga shorts that barely cover my rear end and a lime-green sports bra. While he's distracted by the sight of me half-naked, I take a few quick steps around him and begin cautiously climbing down the rocky side.

"Wait up," he snaps, and reaches for me. "Let me help you."

I glance back at him and see concern in his eyes and something a little darker I don't understand. His hand on my elbow is tight, almost too tight.

"Adam?" I ask, an unspoken question in my eyes.

He shakes the darkness away and takes a deep breath. "Just let me help you."

I frown, and then nod slowly, stepping onto a large boulder while he moves in front of me. I follow him step-by-step onto the rock. The entire time he keeps looking back at me, telling me where to put every step.

The water is so amazingly warm that I moan as soon as I wiggle my toes in it. Adam is already in and the water is just above his knees, about as deep as a hot tub. It doesn't look like it gets any deeper.

"I still can't believe I'm in a hot spring," I say with a large smile on my face as I step in and walk to Adam.

I'm close enough he could wrap his arms around me, but he doesn't.

I don't know if I'm disappointed. Or maybe the heat from the water and the steam is turning my brain to mush.

I take a few steps away from him, peering out over the edge of the water. The magnificence of being surrounded by the mountains calms me like always. I feel a breath full of stress leave me, and my shoulders relax.

I jump when I feel Adam's warm hands on my shoulders, massaging them lightly. He pauses until I relax and then moves them again. His thumb lightly puts pressure on the knots at the back of my shoulders, and my head rolls forward. I bite my bottom lip to hide a moan.

"Just relax," he says softly, and my body listens instantly.

We stand there for who knows how long, as his hands do nothing more than move against my shoulders, relaxing my knots and heating my insides at the same time. I'm about to turn around, to test the power of his kisses again, when I feel his warm breath on my shoulder and the crook of my neck.

His tongue hits my skin first, wetting it lightly, and sends a jolt straight to my stomach, right before his lips press against my skin. I feel the goose bumps ignite all over me and I freeze.

Adam stops and I feel him pull away, but good God, that's the last thing I want him to do now.

I shake my head and whisper, "More," and then his hands are pressing against my shoulders more tightly and his lips are back on my skin.

He kisses a path from my neck down to my collarbone and then back up to the soft flesh behind my ear. I couldn't contain the breathless moan that escapes my lips if I wanted to. And I'm not sure I want to hide my attraction to him anymore.

That slow awakening that occurred earlier in the afternoon has now erupted into an out-of-control wildfire.

I know the only thing that can stop it is more of this—more of Adam's lips on my body and his hands moving to parts that he hasn't yet touched.

"Adam," I breathe out huskily, and turn around so I'm facing him.

He pulls me to him until his arms are wrapped tight against me. My cheek is pressed against his chest and I long to feel his skin beneath his shirt. To feel my hands on him like his hands are on mine, and to see if I wield the same power over him that he does me.

I pull my head back so I'm looking directly at him. He looks at me through hooded lashes as I peer up at him through mine. I don't hide my reaction to him.

Maybe I should.

Maybe I shouldn't want him as badly as I do right now, and maybe this is all going to end up being one big mistake and push us further apart, but I don't care.

My hands go to the edges of his shirt.

I watch him flinch as my hands connect with his hips, lightly brushing across the firm muscle right above the waistband on his shorts, but he doesn't stop me. I push his shirt up, and just as I can't move it anymore, his own hands help me finish pushing it over his head before his hands go back to my hips. I can feel the heat from his skin searing through my own shorts, straight into me as if his fingers are branding me. Claiming me as his.

I lick my lips and press them against his skin.

It's the first kiss I've given him, and my own skin heats as I move my lips slowly against his muscled chest that flexes underneath me. His abs tighten and release, and I feel his fingers dig deeper into my hips, but he doesn't move.

He doesn't pull me to him and take me and he isn't pushing me away.

Every muscle in his body is coiled so tightly that I can see the veins sticking out and running from his wrists all the way up his arms. He's breathing deeply and I'm sure it's matching my own breathing.

"Adam," I say, but it's barely a whisper. It sounds like begging, pleading to my own ears. I don't care. I don't know what's come over me. Maybe the springs are drugged with pheromones and it's only because we're here, in this place and half-naked, that makes me want him so much. He doesn't take his eyes off me.

"Tell me what we did here before."

My eyes move to look over his shoulder. I'm almost ashamed of myself. I don't know this guy—not really—and yet I'm throwing myself at him like a drunken sorority girl. And then the dreams flash in front of me, and my breath hitches. Like Lexi, or Tina, or Britnee.

Oh my God—how many sorority girls were there?

I shake my head and close my eyes at the thought, but Adam's hands tighten on my hips, not letting me move away.

"What is it?"

His voice sounds like an angry growl.

I know without pulling my eyes back to him that he just saw uncertainty and doubt flash all over me. I'm beginning to learn that I can't hide anything from him. It's unnerving how he knows me so well.

"Tell me, Ames."

I blink at the rocks over his shoulder, closing off the thoughts of all the girls. But they don't disappear. Did they all turn to a puddle of mush at Adam's feet?

Of course they did. It's physically impossible to be around him and in his arms without losing your mind and morals.

I shake my head again, unable to look at him. One of his hands leaves my hip and he cups my chin, pulling my eyes to him.

"What did you just see?" His eyes are swirling with lust and need and just a hint of frustration. I don't want to tell him. I don't want the lust to disappear and be replaced with sighs of anger and grinding teeth.

"Nothing."

"You're lying. What is it?"

I sigh and breathe out slowly. My eyes fall to his chest and I almost feel ashamed.

"I was wondering how many girls there were before me."

My voice is as quiet as a mouse. I hate that I'm making him angry when the moment was just so perfect. Adam laughs once, darkly, and my eyes snap back to him.

His other hand comes to my chin and he cups both my cheeks before pressing his lips firmly against mine. It's over before I knew it began, and my lips still feel him when he smiles at me.

"There hasn't been anyone else since the day I saw you on the lawn."

It's not lost on me that he ignores how many women there were before me. I'm not sure it matters anymore. I'm not sure anything matters except the fact that I suddenly don't want Adam's hands to leave my body. Ever.

His touch is like a drug giving me the best high I've ever been on. Not that I've ever tried drugs. At least not that I can remember.

His lips come back to mine, ghosting over my lips with just a hint of a kiss before they land on my ear. His breath gives me shivers.

"I'm not going to tell you what happened here. When I take you again, Ames, it's not going to be like this. Not when you're still doubting so much. The next time I'm inside of you it's going to be when you remember everything, remember how much you love me, and what it's like to be mine. What it's like to be under me and on top of me."

I don't know what he's saying and I don't know if I even asked him a question. All I know is that suddenly I don't doubt him at all. But that's not me talking. I do doubt him. I doubt us. I'm just full of lust and wanting him right now.

I sigh, shaking my head, and know that he's right.

And even though it takes every single measure of control I possess, and then some more, I take a step out of his arms.

"You're right. We should probably go."

∽

My head hurts. How do I stop this? My fingernails dig through the grass and claw at the dirt, trying to find my cell phone. I have to call someone. He can't get away with this. I won't let him.

How dare he think he can do this to me?

Sweat drops into my eyes and I wipe it away with the back of my hand. My hand moves to my jeans to wipe off the sweat and the dirt, but I catch a glimpse of my hand in the moonlight.

I gasp, my body shaking, tears falling down from my eyes instantly. Blood.

I wipe my head again and I cringe at the pain on my cheek and the side of my head that I didn't feel before. When I pull my hand back again, there's more blood.

It's everywhere.

All over my face and on my shirt that is ripped open just above the stomach. My tears fall harder, my sobs grow louder as I try to make it stop, pushing it away from my face, out of my eyes, but it's just making it worse.

"Amy!"

I snap my head in the direction of Adam's voice.

He's running toward me, reaching for me, but as he opens his mouth to yell again, someone jumps on his back, punching him in the side.

Adam leans forward, using his weight to throw the stranger onto the ground. He jumps on the man's chest and raises his fist, punching the guy right in the nose. The man cries out, but Adam doesn't stop.

He uses both fists, punching him over and over again, until the man's head is flopping back and forth. There is no noise coming from him, just the sound of bone hitting bone. It echoes into the night air.

Blood flies everywhere, and yet I can't take my eyes away from him.

Adam turns to me, an evil expression on his face, and then goes back to pummeling the unconscious man on the ground.

He's going to kill him.

Ignoring the pain on the side of my head, I crawl to my feet, forgetting about the phone or getting help.

And then I run.

~

"Damn it! That is not what happened!"

I flinch from the anger in Adam's voice and lean away from him.

My arms are crossed protectively across my chest, and if I lean any farther away from him, my chair will tip over. I'm shaking. The dream is terrifying.

I woke up yesterday morning sweating and screaming so loud that Adam came rushing into my bedroom, his eyes wide and feral. I scrambled to the corner of the bed and threw my hands out.

With tears rushing down my face, I screamed at him to leave me the hell alone.

He looked broken as he stood there, unable to help me, but obviously wanting to.

But I could only see Adam's fists flying and blood from an unknown man splattering him all over his face.

He didn't even notice.

We were doing so well. We had such a good week on our date for lunch and on the hike. We even spent time watching movies together and laughing at the same parts.

And then the dream ruined it all.

Dr. Jamison turns to us, hands clasped softly in her lap. She looks at me and her eyes soften. "Amy, I know this is difficult. I know you're scared and confused, but you said yourself that you had a really good week with Adam before this dream. Should we talk about that first?"

I shake my head, staring out at the once-again-empty playground.

Dr. Jamison presses on. "Tell me about the picnic." My foot starts tapping quickly, nervously, of its own accord. I hear Adam sigh and I flinch when his elbow touches mine.

"Amy," she says, her voice more firm, and I drag my gaze away from the sad-looking abandoned swing set. "Tell me about the picnic. You can do this."

I focus on her green-and-yellow tie-dyed shirt that she has paired with an orange ruffled skirt that drags on the floor.

"He took me to some hot springs."

Dr. Jamison gives me an encouraging nod and I look at Adam. His head is down and his hands are gripping the armrests. I know he's trying to calm down. I remember the picnic and the steam of the water, the way it felt against my skin in the brisk air, and the kiss. Because of all the things that happened that day, Adam's kisses were the best.

"It was nice."

Adam turns to me hesitantly.

Dr. Jamison smiles. "Why was it nice?"

I stare at the ceiling.

One hundred and fifty-two tiles line the ceiling. I count them at every appointment and find comfort in knowing some things will never change.

I inhale slowly, blowing out my breath. I can sense Adam tense next to me.

"Because we didn't talk about us. We just talked about . . . regular stuff." I shrug my shoulders but can feel the backs of my eyes begin to burn.

"What else made it a good day?" Dr. Jamison is smiling, as if she already knows every thought in my head.

My cheeks flush, remembering.

Slick skin, toned abs, wet hair . . . it all flashes to my mind in an instant, and my cheeks heat and my thighs pull together.

"We swam." I sound like a five-year-old speaking basic sentences. Can Adam hear the lust in my voice? I bite the inside of my cheek to keep my smile away.

"And how did you feel when you did that? Did Adam touch you?"

I nod. I focus harder on the hem of her orange skirt, too embarrassed to know what Adam will see in my eyes if I look at him. I run my hands to my ponytail holder, shaking out my hair.

It blocks my view from Adam and his view of my hot pink cheeks. My face feels like it's on fire.

I pull my eyes to Dr. Jamison and she smiles at me victoriously. "You trusted him."

Adam sighs when I nod and from the corner of my eye I see his fingers stretch out from his grip on the armchair.

"And do you think that man . . . the man you spent the day with, trusting, and holding on to, is capable of what you think your dream showed you?"

The man's head flops on the ground as Adam punches him in the face and his blood flies, landing on my already bloody lap.

I freeze in my chair. My back is as straight as a piece of wood and my body is equally as stiff.

The blood.

There was blood everywhere . . . on me. He just wouldn't stop punching him.

Without thinking, my fingers fly to my temple and I find the bump. I have a scar in the same place from that night. It's an older scar, just over an inch long, and slightly hidden in my hairline. I might never have noticed it if I hadn't spent hours over the last several weeks staring at myself in the mirror trying to remember everything.

I gasp.

I turn to Adam.

He looks at my hand on the side of my head and quickly turns away from me. His eyes close and his face falls. He can't even look at me.

Who hurt me that night?

She doesn't wait for me to answer, but I can feel the tension in the room increase as if someone just turned it up on a control panel. Instead, she turns to Adam.

"Tell me what happened that night."

Adam looks at me and purses his lips. His body is as tense as mine and there's anger in his eyes—a wild look that I have never seen before.

"He hurt her." He chokes over the words, and looks away from me, staring at the ugly purple-speckled carpet.

"What do you mean, 'he hurt her'?"

Adam runs his fingers through his hair, linking them behind his neck, before pulling them apart and flexing his fingers. I can feel the tension increasing in his body with every movement.

"I was supposed to pick her up from the library when it closed at ten, but I was running late. She tried calling me, but my phone was dead, so she started walking. Jared attacked her. He . . ." Adam looks at me, and I can see something . . . pain, possibly, in them. He shakes his head, exhaling out a huff of breath.

"What did he do, Adam?"

My skin is crawling. How can everything I see be so horribly wrong?

Adam shakes his head. He stands up so quickly that his chair falls to the floor with a crash. It makes both me and Dr. Jamison jump in our seats.

My eyes are wide open as Adam paces back and forth before stopping, staring at both of us.

His eyes are evil.

"I can't talk about this." He turns, leaves the room, and slams the door.

I am too stunned to move. We both watch the door.

Is he coming back? Do I go to him?

"He isn't the man who hurt you." Her voice is so confident it makes me frown.

"That's not what I was thinking," I snap, too afraid to tell her that's exactly what I'm thinking. Jared had no reason to hurt me. We were friends.

She nods, but she knows I'm lying. I've always sucked at it.

"He loves you."

I feel like someone just grabbed my head and shook my brain, rattling it. Did she not just see what happened? Or maybe she's more stoned than usual.

Adam can flip his temper from calm and cool to the anger of a lion hunting down prey with the flick of a switch.

"He scares me," I whisper, staring at the door, still trying to understand.

"He's hurting and I know this is difficult for you. You're the one who can't remember." She says it calmly, and I feel her hand on my lap. "But you're forcing him to relive every single bad decision the man has ever made, and it's hard to see his failures through the eyes of the woman he loves. Give him some time, Amy. And give yourself some—everything will work out the way it's supposed to."

My feet move, and I don't look back at her.

By the time I'm in the parking lot, Adam's car is gone. I climb into mine, determined to follow him this time.

I have the right to answers when it comes to my own body at the very least.

ELEVEN

It doesn't take me long to find him once I hit The Library. Zander smiles at me from behind the bar as soon as I walk in, nodding his head in Adam's direction. He's in a booth at the back of the bar, hunched over, two beers already at the table.

"Thanks, Zander." He throws a wet towel over his shoulder and rests his elbows on the bar. With a finger wiggle, he waves for me to come closer.

"Not a problem, girl. Just go easy on him, will ya?" He glances around me, over to Adam, and then back to me. His voice lowers by at least an octave. "That night wasn't easy on him."

I nod, not understanding, but determined to find out.

He slides me an opened bottle of 318 Ale and frowns. "He loves you, Amy. A lot. All of this—your accident, the coma, not knowing if you were going to make it . . . and now, just not knowing . . . it's killing him. It's killing all of us. We just want you back, you know?"

"I'm so sorry this has been tough on you."

Zander rolls his eyes, not humored by my sarcasm. "That's not what I meant." He pauses and pushes off the bar, taking a step back before looking back at me. His lip piercing catches the light from above him and sparkles a little bit. It almost makes me smile.

Nothing about Zander, with his dark-as-night eyes and inked-everywhere skin, should be sparkly.

"I know you don't remember me, but I'm not the fuckup I look like. And that guy over there, draining his beers because he just had to relive one of the scariest nights of his life? Well, he's the only one who has ever had my back." He shakes his head and when he speaks again, his voice is softer. Kinder. "I can't imagine what it's like to wake up and be in your place. It's gotta be scary as hell, I get it. But Adam's good people. And he didn't give you that scar on the side of your head that you're rubbing with your shaky little finger."

I drop my hand, not even aware I was doing it.

Zander grins, but it looks out of place on him. Like he doesn't do it often.

I grab my beer without another word because what is there to say to someone who looks like he could eat me for breakfast and spit out my bones?

Adam sits up straighter in his chair when he sees I'm just a couple of tables away and headed straight for him.

"Hey," I say, sliding into the bench across from him.

He closes his eyes and mindlessly peels back the label on the beer bottle in front of him, which has a matching blue label to mine, with 318 printed vertically.

I take a sip, smiling at the taste. I don't generally like beer, but this isn't too bad. Nice, refreshing a little bit.

"It's your favorite beer." Adam nods toward the beer in his hand and then to Zander behind the bar. "When Zander started working here, we came in one night and you made him give you a sample of every beer they have until you could find one you didn't think tasted like Miller Lite keg beer."

I wrinkle my nose. One too many frat parties by the end of my freshman year and I had refused to take another sip of beer. That I remember. This story, I don't, but I don't take my eyes off Adam as he stares at the bar with a distant look on his face.

I examine the label as if it's the only lifeline between us right now. "It's a good beer."

Adam raises his beer in the air, signaling for another round, and looks everywhere besides at me. The uncomfortableness we had just started breaking down increases to insane levels. I feel like I could just . . . snap . . . at any second. Adam looks even closer to the breaking point.

His hands grip the beer so tightly I think it might shatter when he notices me absentmindedly fingering the scar on my hairline.

"I was late that night." He squeezes his eyes shut and shakes his head as if clearing away a nightmare.

My hands freeze on the table. I don't want to move or distract him for a second. Finally, I might get some answers.

"The school library was closed and locked by the time I got there. I was so upset. I was mad at you for leaving the library to walk across the campus alone, mad at Zander for talking me into playing another round of Walking Dead, and mad at myself for not charging my cell phone. When I took off for your apartment, I was just pissed. At everyone. And scared. It was so dark and campus was so empty. Nothing felt right that night."

He shakes his head again and stares at me but without seeing me. Maybe staring through me to the girl who used to love him. I have no idea, but I stay still, listening, not even sure if I'm breathing.

"He was on top of you." He drains the remainder of his beer in one long gulp.

What? My fingertips press against my scar, and Adam flinches when he sees me.

"He hurt you, Amy. Not me. I heard you screaming not far from the tower in the middle of campus. I found you behind the pine trees. Jared was . . . he was on top of you. Hurting you."

I swallow slowly, trying to absorb his words, but not understanding. Or not wanting to. Adam . . . Jared. Jared was my friend. We were both finance majors and had a lot of classes together. He was always so nice to me.

He wouldn't hurt me.

"He was so nice," I mutter, and then lurch back when I realize my mistake. Adam's eyes glow a similarly evil expression. I shake my head quickly and raise a hand. "That's not what I mean. I'm not saying I don't believe you, I just . . . I remember Jared and he was so nice to me."

"Do you?"

I frown. "Do I what?"

"Do you believe me?"

I blink. Unsure. And then nod.

I can see the pain of what reliving this night has done to him, and the sincerity in Zander's eyes at the bar.

At the very least, I don't think Adam hurt me that night.

Relief washes over him and his shoulders sag down. Adam falls back into the booth.

"When did it happen?" I ask, not because it's important or changes anything, I just need to know.

"Spring semester, near the end of our junior year."

"What happened to Jared?"

Adam's nose twitches and then he grins. "He left and never came back. He had a couple of fractured cheekbones and his nose was broken, but nothing too permanent. He never said what happened to him, probably knowing what we would say about him."

≈

"Zander said you might need me." Kelsey smiles and slides in next to me, throwing an arm around me and pulling me close.

I didn't even see her coming until her voice broke through the silence at our table.

"Here's what we're going to do," she says, ignoring the tension between Adam and me.

Zander appears out of nowhere with a round of beers, four shot glasses, and a bottle of tequila. He sits down next to Adam.

Kelsey grins. "A new version of 'I have never.'"

I roll my eyes. I was never good at "I never" . . . the drinking game where someone says something they've never done. If you've done it, you have to take a drink. I always ended the game sober while everyone else involved was trashed.

"I hate that game."

"Yes, but there's a twist to tonight's game," she says, smiling, as if everything is just bright and sunny in her little world. Her happy smile looks almost as strange as Zander's smile. "We're going to say something and you have to guess whether or not it's true. If you're wrong—you drink."

"So this game is called 'make Amy puke her brains out'?"

"Not if you're a good guesser." She smirks and nudges me with her shoulder.

Adam smiles and shakes his head, taking a long pull of his beer.

I watch his Adam's apple dip in his throat, unable to take my eyes off him. How can I go from being so afraid of him to turned on by such a simple movement?

"I'll go first," Zander says. He leans forward with his elbows on the table, and I peel my eyes away from Adam's throat. "You streaked butt naked through our frat house."

Adam snorts and shakes his head. When he drags his eyes to mine, he smiles.

I didn't.

There's no way I did that.

I look to Kelsey to see if she's giving anything away, but she has one hell of a poker face.

"No way," I say confidently, but then jump in my seat when Kelsey smacks her hand on the table and shouts, "Yes!"

"You're lying."

"No," she shouts again, laughter bubbling up from her. "You totally did. Like half the guys in the house saw you."

I look across the table.

Zander looks pleased and pours me a shot. I take it without the help of salt or limes and cringe as it burns my throat.

"I don't believe you." I shake my head. There's absolutely no way I would willingly streak through a frat house.

"Technically," Adam finally says with a shit-eating grin on his face. He pauses and takes a shot with me. "You walked out of my room to go to the bathroom, but you were so drunk you forgot there was still a party going on."

I feel the heat rise on my cheeks, embarrassed that not only does Adam mention me being naked in his room at his frat house, which can only mean one thing, but also at the idea of how many people saw me doing a naked, drunk-stumbling walk.

"Relax, girl." Zander smirks. "There was only like six of us at a room at the end of the hall. But it was the best night of our lives."

"Oh my God." I drop my head into my hands, elbows propped on the table, and bounce against Kelsey's shoulder when she shoves me again.

I point my finger at Zander. "You lied. You should take a shot, too. That isn't streaking."

He shrugs. "Close enough."

Shit.

The rest of the night continues almost the exact same way.

I learn that I dumped a beer all over Lexi's little football cheerleader uniform after Adam and I had been dating a year and she tried to kiss him right in front of me. My first rock concert was Radiohead in Colorado Springs—which I guessed right—remembering the way Adam looked the day he told me about them in the car.

I have never skinny-dipped, which answered a few lingering questions about what exactly I've done in the hot springs.

I not only wore jeans to Thanksgiving dinner at my parents' house, but I skipped Christmas last year altogether after they learned I was moving out of my apartment and in with Adam. That one made me frown and I took two shots because it was too close to all the unanswered questions I still don't understand.

But when I open my mouth to ask them, my tongue feels heavy and too big for my mouth.

"Did we go home to your parents' house then?" I immediately, even in my tequila-induced haze, wish I would have kept my mouth shut.

Adam's eyes go cold like they did the day at the park, and Zander makes a similar expression.

I'm too drunk to think straight.

"Have I ever met them?" I ask again, pushing, because why not? The last two hours have been spent with me learning that I was almost raped by a friend and reliving every embarrassing moment of my life.

Which has been great. I'm happy tonight, if the evidence of my cheek-hurting smile is any clue.

I like this Amy.

I like who I am when I'm at this table with my best friend and the guys I don't remember. Tonight, with liquor warming my veins and my cheeks hurting from laughing so hard, I don't even care that I don't remember them.

What does matter is that no matter what I'm forced to remember and think of—Adam never talks about himself.

"No, you haven't," he says, and throws back a shot. "What else haven't you done?"

I don't let him change the subject, even though I can see the anger dancing across his eyes, warning me to drop it. "Why don't you talk about them?"

"Because his dad's an asshole." Zander fills a shot glass and slides it toward Adam. Almost as if he's helping him ease his pain. I don't get it, but I want to.

I want to understand everything about him. And not because I'm drunk or because I don't remember, but because I *want* to.

"Because I don't." And then he pushes Zander out of the booth's bench and stalks off to the bathroom.

Whatever. He'll have to tell me sometime if he wants me to trust him.

I throw back a shot of Patrón and feel the bar tip to the left and right before straightening out. I blink once, then twice, clearing the haze and blurred edges from my eyes.

I may need to stop drinking.

I listen vaguely to Zander and Kelsey talking, but I'm no longer paying attention. I'm trying to focus my eyes on one particular spot so the room stops spinning.

And I wonder—what would it feel like to be touched by Adam again? The caresses from Adam have teased my skin and I'm a lying ball of crap if I say I don't miss the connection.

I feel my skin heat at the thought of what Adam told me at the hot springs, about how he won't sink into me again until I'm sure.

I'm sure, tonight. I want him. Or maybe it's the liquor.

I don't care.

My body is telling me something completely different from my mind, something I'm learning is a normal occurrence when Adam is so close by.

But maybe it's always been this way. Maybe he's always made me lose my mind, and right now is no different.

I look up in the direction of the bar and see Adam. My eyes narrow, drinking in the profile of him; dark washed jeans with bling on the back pockets that hang off his hips and his butt in a sexy, but slightly messy, way. His pale blue T-shirt stretches across his arms and his back.

I watch him raise his arm. And squeeze onto a woman's bicep.

How did I not notice her before? Now she's all my slightly blurred vision can see as Adam wraps his hand around her arm and pulls her close, whispering something in her ear and smiling.

He's smiling. And holding her.

It's an intimate touch that tells me not only does he know her, but he knows her well. I so rarely see him smile, but he flashes her a large grin and the girl he's touching throws her head back.

I watch her waist-long dirty-blond hair fly out behind her while she laughs. Her eyes practically sparkle as she looks at him and then leans back in.

Kissing him? Telling him something? What in the hell is he doing only fifteen feet away from me in a bar, touching and holding and laughing with someone?

"Who is that?" I snap, and narrow my eyes.

Kelsey and Zander both stop whatever conversation they were having. They turn in the direction of where I'm trying to light Adam on fire with my eyes.

It's part jealousy and part drunkenness.

Who am I kidding? It's all jealousy and anger.

Why is it every freaking time I begin to trust him—to begin to want him—he pulls something like this? I flip through my memories in my dreams—Lexi, Tina, Britnee . . .

Always, there's another girl in his arms as soon as he walks away from me. Seeing it happen in person is more painful than I could have imagined. More painful than I remember seeing in my dreams.

"I don't know," Kelsey whispers quietly, looking nervously at Zander.

He shrugs, unaffected. I want to kick him in the shins.

"Well find out," I snap, and take another shot, relishing the burn in my throat.

"Calm down, Amy. It's totally innocent."

I shoot daggers out of my eyes at my best friend. "Lexi, Tina, Britnee," I count off, holding up a finger for each girl I *do* remember. "How many other girls were there that he held and hugged and kissed when we were dating and so easily brushed it off with a plausible excuse?"

My blood is beginning to boil. Maybe it's the alcohol making me irrational. I don't know.

I also don't care.

I also ignore the fact that no one bothers answering my question.

But then Adam turns and smiles at me. I see his arm let go of the girl next to him as he faces me from across the bar.

I blink.

$\sim$

"Here's to finals being done. Cheers!" Kelsey lifts her shot glass in the air and I raise mine along with Zander and Adam. It's freezing cold out tonight; the snowstorm hit Denver just as our statistics final finished. Kelsey met the three of us at The Library for some end-of-the-semester celebrating, which has quickly dissolved into a game of "get Amy as plastered as possible."

"Quarters!" I shout, the one word turning into four syllables as it rolls over my heavy and numb tongue.

Adam laughs and puts an empty cup in the middle of the table. "Tired of being the only drunk one?" He kisses my cheek and I nudge him sideways with my shoulders.

"I have to get the advantage somehow."

His eyes rake over my entire body sitting next to him in the booth. I don't know what he sees. In his black, hooded sweatshirt, my unwashed hair thrown up into a bun, and my gray yoga pants, I don't look attractive at all. But Adam looks at me like he did this morning when he woke me up, naked, and made us so distracted we were almost late for our finals.

I feel naked under his hooded gaze, like I always do, as one of his eyebrows quirks up into a playful expression.

"I'd let you take advantage of me anytime."

"It's not taking advantage if you're willing," I remind him, saying the same thing he's said to me many times since we began dating.

"Gah! Enough, you sex fiends," Kelsey scolds us from across the table, but it's not like she and Zander are any different.

"Okay." I slam my palms on the table and then reach for the quarter Adam is holding between his thumb and forefinger. I state the rules even though they're not necessary; there's only one. "Miss a shot, take a shot."

I ping the quarter off the wooden table and it lands directly into the empty glass.

We go around the table and everyone misses except me. Who knew I would be so good at quarters? I make them play it all the time because no one beats me. Ever.

～

The memory fades and I blink my eyes. When I shake my head, clearing my mind, Adam is back at the table next to me with a worried expression on his face.

"Are you okay?" Adam asks, and lightly squeezes my hand underneath the table. I look around the bar and the girl he was talking to is hanging all over some other guy. Kelsey is now sitting next to Zander and both are eyeing me cautiously.

The warmth of his hand feels exactly the same way I imagined it felt in my memory. Maybe it's the liquor coursing through my veins that makes me no longer care about whatever girl Adam has ever been with. Maybe it's the fact that even if I don't remember everything, I'm beginning—finally—to remember Adam, and he isn't as sketchy as I originally believed he was.

Maybe it's just because I'm horny and Adam is sexy as sin with his jet-black hair that falls haphazardly around his ears, a little bit messed up from the long day, and all I can think about is running my fingers through it, pulling him to me, and feeling his lips against mine.

"Yeah," I say, a little bit breathlessly and then smile mischievously. "You guys all suck."

I point at each of them and when they don't respond, I dig through my wallet, dragging out a quarter.

Then I clear off a clean space on the shot-glass-littered table in front of me.

Adam throws his head back and laughs. "That's what you just remembered?" he asks when he sees the silver coin in my hand.

I smirk at all of them, looking across the table at Kelsey and Zander, who both groan.

"Miss a shot, take a shot." I bounce the quarter on the table, and just like in my vision, it hits the wood and bounces into the shot glass I left in the center of the table.

I clap my hands, cheering excitedly. I continue laughing as every single one of them miss when it's their turn. Adam throws his arm around my shoulder after he misses his second shot and pulls me to him, his hand feeling warmer than normal against my skin.

He presses his lips against my temple softly and whispers into my ear, "I hate this fucking game."

I lift my chin, looking up at him, and see the same heated expression I saw in my memory. "That's because you always lose."

Kelsey smiles widely at me from across the table, clearly happy that I've remembered something good.

TWELVE

L et me help you," Adam rasps out in a deep voice that I'm not sure I've heard before. His hands cup my shoulders as he gently steadies me on the edge of the bed.

"I'm fine," I slur, swaying back and forth. Adam chuckles and bends down on his knees in front of me. His head drops as he begins unbuckling the straps on my heels. My ankles and feet are killing me from walking home from The Library where we left Zander and Kelsey. Neither of us was okay to drive, and we don't live far, so I leaned against Adam the entire walk home.

He kept an arm around my waist, holding me to him, letting me inhale his cologne that smells spicy and masculine and has only served to increase my lust for him.

I don't care that I'm drunk. I have a desire to connect with him other than in the cloudy memories.

"I had fun tonight."

I stare down at him when he looks up at me from his position on the floor. He's in between my legs, massaging my ankle.

His lips turn up into a smile and he takes a deep breath. I can see his struggle to allow me my space, to give me time, but I don't want it anymore.

Not tonight.

I raise my hand and his body freezes.

His eyes watch as my fingers gently push back some of the hair that has fallen onto his forehead. He inhales a quick breath while I exhale slowly, my fingers slightly shaking. His hair is softer and thicker than I thought it would feel as I let it slide through my hands.

One of his hands reaches up and grabs on to my wrist. His lips press a gentle kiss on the pulse point and he holds it to his lips for longer than necessary.

I'm frozen in time, the only sound in the room is the increased breathing between both of us. I bite the inside of my cheek, thinking—hoping—he's going to continue kissing up my arm and to my neck, where I already know what it feels like to have his unshaven scruff scratch against my sensitive skin.

But he doesn't.

Instead, he lowers my hand to my lap. His eyes are full of regret when he shakes his head.

"I can't do this, Amy. Not when you're drunk."

He leans back so he's sitting on his heels and stares at me, watching me for acceptance.

I refuse to give it to him.

"It's not taking advantage if they're willing," I whisper, repeating back to him what I remembered from just a few hours earlier.

I see his strength crack slightly as he stands up and leans over me. I raise my chin, staring him straight in the eyes when his hands cup my chin. His strong hands hold me gently as he peers into my face, debating what to do.

"I love you too much to hurt you . . ." His voice trails off and his eyes close tightly. His fingers twitch against my skin. I want to ask him what else he was going to say, but then he opens his eyes and stares at me, determined. "I can't hurt you."

"Please," I say, reaching out to take hold of his wrists. I feel his pulse beneath my fingers and I know it's faster than it should be.

"Let me feel you. You said it's what we've always done best. I need this tonight."

I stand up and take a step closer to him, my chest brushing lightly against his, and I hear him grind his teeth together.

"Ames."

"Please, Adam."

I pull his hands off my cheeks and then I slowly lift my fitted, vintage Eagles shirt over my head and drop it on the floor at our feet.

Adam watches it fall to the ground and slowly drags his eyes over my body and my naked chest, surprised that I wasn't wearing a bra.

His hands grip my hips and he pulls me to him, my breasts hitting the soft blue shirt he's still wearing.

I want to rip it off and feel his skin against mine, but I know I can't push him too far or else he'll leave. And this is the first time I haven't wanted him to go anywhere.

Not now.

His tongue darts out and I watch him lick his lips before he frowns, still fighting what I can see he so clearly wants.

"You can't hate me in the morning for this."

I don't answer. Mostly because I can't.

This could be the biggest mistake I've ever made, but I don't want to stop now.

I feel exactly like I did in every memory I remember having. Being around Adam makes me feel completely out of control and it's the first time it hasn't scared the hell out of me.

I feel empowered. Like everything he's told me is true and with him I can be anybody I've ever wanted, but mostly I can be myself.

"Kiss me," I say softly, and watch his resolve break.

He pulls me even closer to him so there isn't a single place we're not connected. I can feel everything. His shirt against my skin, the roughness of his jeans pressing against my legs, and one hand leaves my hip, gripping the back of my neck tightly.

Our lips meet in a passion that is unparalleled to anything I've experienced in my life. I was expecting timidity from him, but instead I feel a confidence and a desperation pouring into me as I open my mouth and curl my tongue against his, accepting him willingly.

My hands grab the back of Adam's head and I pull him closer to me, telling him that I want this, and I revel in the groan that escapes his lips.

He ends the kiss abruptly and I hold on to him, afraid that he's going to change his mind, and I don't know why, but I can't let that happen.

Not tonight.

Not now when, for the first time since I've woken up from my coma, I feel like maybe this is where I really belong.

With him.

"On the bed."

My eyes snap to his. His eyes are almost completely black. The commanding order takes me by surprise, and I freeze, suddenly nervous.

He doesn't smile. He doesn't do anything except let go of my body. I shiver when the warmth of his hands leaves me.

"What?" I shift back and forth on my feet, nervous.

Or I sway because of the alcohol. I'm not sure.

He doesn't say anything else as he pulls his shirt at the back of his neck and takes it off, dropping it onto the floor next to mine.

"Lay down, Amy."

My lips twitch to argue back, but something in me doesn't want to.

For the first time, a voice inside I've never heard tells me to trust him. That he'll take care of me and that he won't hurt me.

I unzip my skirt and do what I'm told, slowly moving back to the bed, and lay down in the center.

I watch Adam squeeze his hands into fists and then stretch his fingers out. His breathing is heavy as he stands on the side of the bed watching me, and my skin lights up with goose bumps from head to toe.

"I can't take advantage of you tonight," he says with a deep rumble in his voice and begins slowly climbing over me.

He braces himself up on his hands, his knees in between my legs, pushing my knees apart. He still has his jeans on and the roughness of the denim against my sensitive skin makes my legs tremble. "But I can make you feel good."

A whimper escapes my mouth.

I stare at him, my lips parted and my breathing ragged.

"God, you're beautiful," he whispers against my lips when he lowers his mouth and gently brushes his lips over mine. I reach up to press against him harder, but he pulls away, smirking.

He shakes his head. "Let me give this to you tonight."

I'm about to ask him what he means, but then his hand leaves the bed next to my head and he presses into the skin of my abdomen.

My breath hitches and I raise my head to kiss him again. I want to taste him, to become familiar with him, even though I don't understand why.

Not completely.

But he doesn't let me do it.

His head is bent down and he's watching his own hand roam slowly across my stomach. His fingers graze over my healing, large scar on the right side of my stomach, and he drops his head to my chest.

His hand stills on me, and I bring one of my hands up, running my hand through his hair.

"It's okay," I whisper against him.

It's not and we both know it.

He shakes his forehead against my chest and I feel his hot breath on my breast as he exhales loudly.

I shift under him, my body burning, and I try to pull my legs together to relieve some sort of the pressure that's down there, but I can't because his legs are in the way.

All I do is shift against his hardness and Adam lets out a low groan.

I think it's because he's as turned on as me, but then he raises his head and stares me straight in the eyes.

He's just inches from me and his hand brushes against my scar again.

"I can't do this to you." He presses his lips to mine quickly, but his eyes have already gone cold. "Good night, Amy."

My eyes widen and I gasp. "Adam."

My hand on the back of his head tightens. I try to pull him toward me, but he's too strong.

He pulls away and climbs off the bed, reaching down only to grab his shirt off the floor, and then the door to my room slams shut.

It all happens before I can understand why. I don't understand the look of disgust he gave me when his hand touched my scar or why he suddenly seemed angry and frustrated.

I fall asleep with tears falling down my cheeks, not caring that my mascara is going to be all over my pillow and sheets in the morning.

He just left me—naked and wanting him for the first time in as long as I can remember—without any sort of explanation as to why. And I hate the feeling eating at me, like I've done something wrong or disappointed him in some way.

~

When I wake up in the morning, my eyes are so sore and swollen I can barely manage to crack them open. When I do, I roll over in my bed and stare at my closet door.

The door was left wide open before we left for the bar last night and I cringe at the mess I left on the floor. All my dresses that I bought at the mall with Kelsey hang in the middle. The bright colors are completely opposite the surrounding clothes I've apparently bought over the last two years.

It's as if the "old clothes" are mocking me for even trying to think they would still fit my skin, or me, the way they used to. The way they did when I tried to pretend to be someone my parents wanted me to be.

If I've learned anything in the last couple of weeks, it's that reality that sinks into my bones and feels truer than anything else I know.

And now I just need to figure out who I became once I had the freedom to do so.

In order to do that, I not only need answers from Adam about last night, which embarrasses me and makes my eyes burn all over again just thinking about how he left me alone without any explanation, but I also need answers about everything.

Who is he? Who am I? What happened to me?

And I have to get them before something else tears us away from one another.

I throw on yoga shorts and a baggy T-shirt in search for answers and pain-reliever meds for my tequila-induced headache.

I ignore the shirt on my floor that I threw down last night in order to try to get Adam in my bed.

Maybe it was too soon.

Or maybe the thought of looking at and touching my scarred abdomen disgusts him.

The thought makes me pause at the door. I rest my head against the cool wood and take a deep breath. Is that what that was?

Do my scars and the thought of touching me now turn him off?

My legs are shaking, a mixture of dehydration and nerves, and I take another deep breath when I hear voices coming from the kitchen.

One distinctly Adam.

The other is female. A girl?

Looking at my clock, I see that it's already ten in the morning. Not only did I sleep in longer than I usually do, but there's a girl in my apartment the very night after I was rejected.

I open the door slowly, not wanting to interrupt the visitor, and trying not to become upset until I know what's going on.

Jesus. When did I become such a neurotic, emotional girlfriend who constantly thinks their boyfriend is cheating on her? Why is that always my first assumption when it comes to Adam?

I blow out a frustrated breath and then I laugh to myself when the girl makes a frustrated growl on her own.

A growl that can only come from Kelsey.

I tiptoe down the hall, not meaning to eavesdrop, but wondering why she would be here so early on a day when we don't have anything planned.

Her soft but scolding voice makes me freeze in the hallway. I plaster my back against the wall as I hear her clearly punctuated words—a sure sign she's pissed and trying not to yell.

"You have to tell her," she says to Adam. "Everything. She deserves to know everything."

Adam lets out a frustrated sigh. "You know why I can't, Kels. The doctor said any news could shock her and make everything take longer."

"It's already taking too long. She has the right to know."

"It's too soon." I can hear his anger with her.

If I could see him, I have no doubt that his hands would be clenched into fists or he'd be grabbing tufts of his hair at the nape of his neck.

"You tell her," she growls, "or I will."

"It's none of your business, Kelsey. This is between me and her."

Which I take as my cue because I'm beyond upset at hearing this conversation that doesn't make any sense but is enough to make all sorts of scary ideas run through my head.

"Tell me what?"

I walk around the corner, hands crossed over my chest, and glare at my best friend and my boyfriend.

Both of whom tell me they love me, but are clearly hiding something that shouldn't be hidden.

They turn to me and their mouths drop open.

No one says anything so I stomp around them and pour myself a cup of coffee. I take my first sip and close my eyes, growing more impatient by the silence.

Without looking at them, I dig through the cupboards until I find our bottle of pain meds and pop two into my mouth.

"What is it?" I snap, my eyes darting between both of them.

They say nothing, but Kelsey looks embarrassed and glances down at her feet. Adam can't, or won't, look me in the eyes either. There's a faint pink color on his cheeks like he's embarrassed or ashamed of just getting busted for something he shouldn't have been doing.

Or maybe he's embarrassed about leaving me in my room naked and unsatisfied.

But whatever.

I can't take any more of this bullshit. I leave the kitchen, not looking at either of them.

Twenty minutes later, I'm showered and dressed for a day at Hooka Joe's, wearing the name-branding T-shirt and a short denim skirt. I don't have to be at work, but it gives me an excuse to get out of the apartment and not spend the day suffocating under the tension.

When I reach the kitchen, Adam is at the table, staring blankly at his hands. Kelsey is gone.

"It isn't what you were thinking."

I pause and turn to him. He doesn't raise his head to look at me.

I make a disgusted grunting sound and press my keys tightly into the palm of my hand. The metal presses into my palm until it stings, but I don't care.

"You don't know what I was thinking."

He snorts. I roll my eyes. We're back to our typical responses to one another. Awesome.

"I'm not cheating on my best friend with your best friend."

My eyes widen. Does he really think I lack *that* much trust in him?

"That's really not it at all, Adam. I just don't know what to think. And I'd like to know what you two were talking about."

He shakes his head, and yet, still doesn't look at me. "I can't tell you."

I smack my lips together. "Right. Of course not. Heaven forbid someone actually tells me what in the hell is going on around here. You know, it's just my life we're talking about, no big deal."

He slams his hands down on the table. His full mug of coffee shakes and spills out over the top.

"Do you have any idea how hard this is for me? I love you and I would die for you. I had to watch you!"

At my gasp, Adam takes a deep breath, running both hands down his face as if he's trying to erase a memory.

My memory . . . the one thing I want answers to.

"I sat there with you, waiting, not sure if you'd make it. I was the one who didn't leave your bed while your parents went on their cruise, and you don't remember one fucking thing of the good. You sit here, every day, cursing me for my mistakes . . ." He pauses and inhales a deep breath. I can do nothing except sit, frozen to my seat, with my jaw hanging to the floor. "And there was way more good than shitty, Ames."

I jump at the sound of his coffee mug slamming into the porcelain sink. I'm surprised it doesn't shatter into a million pieces with the force of his throw.

"God! This just sucks! Don't you think that I want you to *feel* how much you love me? Remember how much I love you?

"And do you know how scared I am—every single fucking day—that you won't? Christ, Ames, we got this place to start a life together . . ." He waves his finger back and forth between the two of us, pausing to take another breath. "Our life together. You wanted it just as much as me, and every day I wake up now, afraid to say the wrong thing, afraid you'll pack up and leave, and afraid you'll never remember all the ways I used to make you smile and laugh. You won't remember the night we made love in here for the first time, before we had furniture. I'm so scared you won't remember any of it!"

His chest heaves up and down, in and out, stretching his skull T-shirt. His hair is a complete mess from running his hand furiously through it.

"I love you, Amy."

His voice is low, calmer. I can't say anything back to him, and I see the pain pierce straight into his heart as I sit here, thinking of what he said: *I had to watch you . . . not sure if you'd make it.*

"I love you more than anything and I began falling in love with you the day I pretended you were smarter than me in statistics, just so I could find an excuse to be alone with you."

Finally, I find my voice. "What do you mean you watched me?"

Confusion flickers across his eyes and then he frowns. "Did you hear anything I just said? I love you, Amy. Please," he pleads with me, begs me, "don't make me relive that day. I can't."

I reach out and touch his hand.

"But I have to know what happened. Just tell me. I can't handle all these things that are confusing me. I need you to tell me."

He shakes his head, running his hand through his hair, and the other gripping mine even tighter. The tension between us is palpable. I can feel it filling the air between us as I try to will him with my eyes to tell me.

I need the truth.

"You fell . . ." he begins, and then his head drops with a shake back and forth. He pulls his hand from mine and turns away from me. "I can't, Amy. You'll remember someday; I know it. But don't ask me to relive it."

I have nothing to say.

We're both silent for minutes or hours. Maybe it's only seconds, but the only sound I can hear is the ticking of a clock on the wall that sounds like a giant gong.

Finally, I ask, "Is that why you wouldn't touch me last night? Does it have to do with my accident and my scar?"

His head snaps to mine, hands on his hips, frown lines running across his forehead.

"What? God, no. You think I don't want that?" he asks, waving toward the direction of my room. "Of course I do. I just couldn't do it last night. Not when you were drunk, not when . . ."

"I don't trust you."

He pulls his bottom lip into his mouth and scrapes it along his teeth. He stares at the pictures on the wall and closes his eyes, breathing heavily.

"You were the first person to trust me. To see past the shit I threw out for everyone else as an act."

"I don't understand what that means, Adam."

His head falls and he takes a seat on the couch, knees spread apart, elbows resting on his knees, and props his head up, running his hands through the back of his hair.

I sit down on a different couch, watching him, forgetting about last night and my coffee, which is cold by now.

This is important. This is real.

Whatever he's struggling with right now will answer so many questions for me.

Finally, he looks at me.

"I know when I started hitting on you that you thought the same thing about me as everyone else did. You saw me as a player, someone who didn't give a shit about anything in life besides partying, hooking up with random girls, and making sure my grades were just good enough to stay on the soccer team." He rubs the back of his neck with one hand and stares out the window. "You weren't wrong; no one was. But you were the first person to look past all that and want to know the real me."

"Who is . . . what?" I ask slowly, not wanting to push him too far.

This is the most Adam has ever opened up to me, and I don't want to miss a single second of it.

"I'm no one special, Ames. I'm just the kid from a fucked-up family, who ran to Colorado, taking the first scholarship that was thrown my way, so I could get away from the hell I lived in." He shrugs. "That day I saw you on the quad, laughing with Tyler? It was the first time I didn't feel like I was drowning in darkness."

He turns to face me and one side of his lips turns up. "I know that sounds cheesy. But that's how it's always been whenever I'm around you. You just . . . erase the darkness in me."

Wow. I exhale a shaky breath. I chew on the inside of my bottom lip, overwhelmed with what I just heard.

"What hell did you come from?"

He closes his eyes and shakes his head.

"Your parents?"

His nose twitches and his fingers fidget in his lap. I know I'm close to something. Understanding him more.

"I can't talk about that now."

"Did you ever tell me?"

He nods and stares out the window with a blank expression. I want to ask him what he's thinking about. The time he told me, or the hell he lived in?

"Will you ever tell me again?" I ask so softly I'm not sure he heard me.

"Yeah," he says slowly and just as softly as I spoke to him. "I never cared about being a good guy before I met you, Amy. I know it's stupid to say you changed me, and maybe it wasn't so much you changing me as much as it was me realizing I wanted to be better for someone. I wanted, for the first time in my life, to do something right. I wanted to make you proud of me."

His eyes fall on every surface in the apartment. He takes it all in, thinking quietly. I give him the silence even though a thousand questions are screaming in my head, wanting to be answered.

"I know this isn't anything like you grew up in. I know our apartment is small and the furniture is shit."

I laugh softly and I watch him smile, staring at the pictures on the far wall. Our mirage. Our life of memories that I don't remember.

He bites the inside of his cheek and purses his lips together.

"But this place . . . this place is the best home I've ever had."

Tears fall down my cheeks quietly. I don't understand why I'm crying, why I'm so moved by what he just said to me, but my heart is breaking for the man who always seems so confident, borderline arrogant.

He sits on the couch, almost afraid to look at me, and all I want to do is go to him, comfort him in some small way.

So I do.

Slowly, I uncurl from the uncomfortable couch that should have been re-covered or thrown into a fire at least ten years ago and walk to him. When I stand in front of him, he sits back on the couch, and without knowing what I'm doing, I fall into his lap.

His arms wrap around me instantly, pulling my legs so I'm cradled in his lap and in his arms. His squeezes me tightly and buries his face into the crook of my neck. I wrap my arms around his neck and hold him close, feeling somehow closer to him in the silence and the wake of his admission than I have since the moment I opened my eyes to the stranger sitting in my room at the hospital almost two months ago.

THIRTEEN

"Did you and Adam get everything worked out?"

I look at Kelsey over the bar at Hooka's. I left Adam a couple of hours ago after we sat on the couch, not saying anything else to one another. I needed my space. I figure he did too since he was dressed for the gym with a pair of boxing gloves draped over one shoulder when I headed out to the coffee shop.

He looked like he had run a marathon, and I realized that even though we may have dated for two years, it was rare for Adam to open up to me the way he did this morning.

It physically drained him.

I felt the same way; which is why I found solace in slugging coffee drinks for the afternoon to a small crowd of artistic types who are probably more hungover than I am.

I lift my shoulders in answer to her question. I still have so many things I need to know, like what she was doing in my apartment this morning. Somehow though, after everything he shared with me this morning, it feels almost like a betrayal to go behind his back and find the answers from Kelsey.

And I realize as I watch my best friend that I *want* to trust Adam. Even when I don't understand everything, or know everything, there is always something in me pulling me back to him.

Wanting to know what he has to say, valuing it more than anyone else, even Kelsey.

"We're okay." I offer a weak smile.

She shuffles back and forth on her feet, mindlessly staring at the muffin case.

"I wanted to explain this morning."

I hold up a hand. "Not necessary."

Her eyes narrow. "But he didn't tell you, did he?"

"I don't know what you were talking about this morning, Kelsey. But, whatever it is, unless you're involved, I don't think I want to know."

"I feel like things are different between us."

She bites her lips and I see the tears in her eyes. I walk around the bar and hug my best friend in the whole world. I wish I could tell her that things are going to be okay, that everything will be fine, but I can't because I don't want to lie.

Something is different between the two of us. Maybe once I remember everything, I'll understand. But for now, there is a divide that can't be closed just because we want it to be.

"It's not your fault, Kels," I tell her, hugging her as both of us begin crying softly. "I feel like I'm not the same. I know I changed and I don't remember it, but I don't think you can go through what I'm experiencing and not be changed by it, too."

She nods into my shoulder, sniffling against my shirt. "I love you."

I pull back from her and wipe my eyes. "I know. And I love you, too. I'm happy that you're with Zander. And I think that once my memories come back, we'll be fine. I just can't make those promises right now."

"I know. I just miss you." She grins, sort of. It's a mix of a grin and a wince. "Oh, I wanted you to know. That girl Adam was talking to last night?"

"Yeah?"

"Zander talked to her after you left. Her name is Melanie and she works with Adam. I just thought you'd want to know who she is."

I don't think it matters, but I thank her anyway.

She leaves to meet up with Zander to hit their favorite hot springs.

My cheeks blush thinking about the last time Adam and I went there. The grin on her face as she leaves and the wiggling of her eyebrows makes me laugh, knowing exactly what they'll be doing there.

~

"What a long day," Preston says as she collapses next to me on a stool at the coffee bar.

It's almost ten o'clock at night and I can't believe that I've been here for almost ten hours already. The day somehow flew by. Maybe it was just because I've been afraid to go back home and see Adam, uncertain of where we go from here.

I'm finishing the final count on the cash register and Preston has just locked the doors and finished cleaning the floor for the night.

"I'm beat." I hide a yawn and begin adding up the credit card receipts.

"There's a band playing tonight at a small rock club just outside Denver. Would you and Adam want to come with me and Benjamin?"

I give her a strange look. "You and Benjamin?"

She laughs. "Yeah, we've been together forever. Since we were kids, practically."

I can't hide my shock, and based on her laugh, she's used to it. "But he's so . . . normal looking."

"Hey!" She slaps me with the towel in her hands and laughs with me. "I'm more than a pierced freak with purple hair."

I know she is, and I know she's teasing. But Benjamin?

He seems so straitlaced. Like he'd prefer a night at the opera or a classical music performance. Preston looks like she belongs in a mosh pit. He's quiet, shy almost. And Preston, well, she's anything but. Talk about opposites attract.

I may be exhausted, but out of morbid curiosity, I want to see them together in public.

"All right," I tell her, and pull out my cell phone. I send Adam a text asking if he wants to go out with Preston and Benjamin for the night.

"You're just going to see what we're like in public, aren't you?"

Heat infuses my cheeks. "Maybe."

She rolls her eyes. "God, you're horrible. You were like this when you first started working here, too. All wide-eyed and nervous to be around me and the stoners who come in. You changed a lot, you know."

I look at my phone to see if Adam responded. Also because this conversation makes me nervous.

Preston never talks about me before the accident.

"How so?" I finally ask.

She looks to the ceiling like she's thinking and plays with her hot-pink-and-purple-striped ponytail. The skulls are gone from her fingertips and replaced with hot-pink daisies.

"You were . . . sad the first day you came in. But yet, I don't know . . . there was something about you that made me want to hire you right away. Like you were trying to experience something new or fighting to get somewhere."

"That's deep." I grin, but my hands are shaking.

Was I always that obvious to everyone who saw me? Just some lost girl walking around following a path she didn't want but not knowing what other road to choose?

"Shut up. It's true, though. How much have you remembered?"

I shrug. "Not much. Not about that anyway. I know my parents and I aren't close anymore. Or, farther apart than we used to be, and I know I turned down the job my dad got for me."

She nods like she knew this.

I'm guessing she did, she and I being best coworker friends and all.

"The day you came in here you threw down your resume and after I looked at it, you pressed your hands on the bar, looked me straight in the eye, and said, 'Listen. I know I don't seem like the type to work in a coffee bar, but I'll be the best manager you could ever hire. I need this job. I need to do something just for me and prove to everyone who wants something from me that I can be successful on my own.'"

My entire body is shaking. I can't believe I would be so bold, but Preston is smiling at me like it was the greatest day of her life.

"What did you say?"

"Welcome to the club."

She hops off the barstool to go finish cleaning the back room, leaving me alone to wonder what she means.

I'm just putting the money into the safe to lock up for the night when my phone vibrates.

Adam: *You sure you want to go with me?*

I know my answer before I have to think about it.

Me: *Yes. How opposite are Preston and Benjamin?*

Adam: *This is going to be fun. I'll be there in ten.*

I close my phone. Then I change into an extra tank top Preston has for me in the back room so I don't have to wear Hooka's plastered across my chest all night long.

⁓

It turns out that Preston and Benjamin aren't that opposite at all. When we show up to People's Bar, where a local heavy rock band is playing, I almost don't recognize him.

He has on black skinny jeans and heavy metal chains hanging from his pockets, black onyx rings on his fingers, a nose piercing that is connected to a chain from his nose to his right ear, and his eyes are lined in a dark black eyeliner. His light blond hair that is usually parted in a preppy way is spiked straight up into the air and out to the sides in clumps. And it's a lime-green color that is completely opposite from Preston's bright colors, yet complementary in the same way. I realize it's probably the perfect metaphor for the entire relationship.

Apparently Benjamin doesn't feel the need to assert his alternative rock personality at all hours of the day, and instead is happier looking like the shy, pretty-boy type when he's at work.

I was totally fooled.

My cheeks turn a dark maroon color, and my chest and neck feel splotchy from the embarrassed heat when everyone turns to me and dies laughing at my shock at seeing his transformation into someone who I would have considered as Benjamin's evil twin brother.

But the night is a blast. We jump around to the earsplitting music that is too loud to really talk over. Adam and I don't touch except for the occasional brush of our hands or legs when we bump into each other. I stick with water, still slightly hungover from the night before, and am pleasantly surprised to see Adam do the same thing.

As the band plays their final song, I take a break from the jumping to lean back against our table and enjoy the night.

My hair is so sweaty it's sticking to my neck, and my tank top is plastered against every inch of my skin. I can even feel the sweat inside my red Doc Martens boots.

But even so, I've been having fun all night, getting lost to the screaming musicians who, even though I don't quite appreciate the type of music, have an incredible sound.

We lost Benjamin and Preston hours ago to the mosh pit down by the front of the stage. Occasionally I've been able to get glimpses of Preston jumping around, but it's felt like Adam and I have been on our own all night.

"You ready to get out of here?" he asks, his breath tickling my ear.

I nod, unsure if I can speak.

When I turn to him, I'm thankful we didn't have any drinks tonight. The pull I felt last night is even stronger when I can feel all my senses.

The callused pads of his fingers as they trail down my arm before lacing our hands together, the smell of his cologne . . . it's so powerful, and I stare at him, nodding, even though I'm no longer sure if he even asked me a question.

He smiles at me like he knows how flustered I am.

And I bet he does.

"Let's go," he says, and tugs me out the door, barely giving me enough time to grab my purse before following him.

FOURTEEN

I kick off my boots and drop my purse on the floor as soon as we get to our apartment and head for the fridge for some water. When I turn around, Adam is standing in front of the windows looking out at the dark night sky with his hands in his front pockets. He looks lost in thought, and I frown, watching him.

He turns to me and rubs his lips together. "I need to tell you something."

I freeze.

The plastic top of the water bottle stops at my bottom lip and I can't take my eyes off him. His face is downcast, staring at the slightly stained carpet, and his shoulders are rounded forward.

"Okay."

"Sit down on the couch."

I bristle at the coldness of his voice, but he doesn't notice.

Adam doesn't look at me at all. He turns back to the windows and stares out in the darkness that is sprinkled with streetlights, but not enough light to really see anything.

I settle on the side of the couch farthest from him and pull my knees up to my chest, hugging them with my arms.

Somehow I feel the need to protect myself from whatever is coming my way.

He blows out a forced breath through his lips and rubs his hands through his hair. I can see him looking at my reflection in the window, but I don't think he's trying to see me. He looks like he's trying to avoid me completely.

When he speaks, his voice breaks, tripping over the words.

"When I was ten, I watched my dad kill my mom."

My mouth drops open and freezes in a perfect O shape. Nerves dance across my skin. I unwrap my arms from my knees, shaking them out, but it doesn't take away the buzzing feeling that's moving all over me.

"What?" I croak, and Adam shakes his head.

Slowly, Adam pulls his eyes to mine as silence falls into every corner of our apartment. He sees the fear written all over my face and I catch a glimpse of a similar look on his own. His voice breaks and from across the open space, I see his eyes fill with tears.

"This is why I didn't want to tell you . . . not when . . ."

"I'm not sure I trust you," I finish for him.

He blanches at my bluntness and then nods. "You thought I hurt you that night. With Jared. How am I supposed to tell you where I come from when you think I'm as evil as the man who created me?"

I bite my bottom lip, trying to find something to say to ease his concern. I can't, though. He's absolutely right.

"Tell me what happened."

He closes his eyes, sighs, and then slowly walks toward me on the couch. I scoot back to the end of the couch until I hit the armrest while he takes a few more steps closer.

He presses his tongue against his teeth then takes a seat on the love seat across from me. I feel both relief and regret as I watch him sit down with such a pained expression on his face.

"My dad was a drunk and he beat my mom. A lot."

He swallows, and I see the ghosts of his past dancing across his eyes.

"He came home one night, blaming her for losing his job. They argued and he threw her down the stairs." Tears drop down his cheek shamelessly, and my feet are moving before I can tell them to stop.

I take a seat next to him, placing my hand over his. He smiles sadly at my hand and then looks me in the eyes.

"She broke her neck and died instantly. He went to prison and my mom's parents took me in."

I squeeze my hand against his, offering him the only small comfort I can.

If it were anyone else, I'd have my arms wrapped around them, but I can't do it.

He looks straight into my eyes, reading my mind.

"I am *not* my dad, Amy. I have a quick-trigger temper, and I may get mad and throw something, but I have not and will never hurt you."

I look down at our hands; the intensity in his eyes is too much for me to handle. I'm calm, I think.

Somehow, even when I'm afraid, his touch has calmed me. But he's also right, because I don't trust him. Not fully.

I don't know how those two things can happen at the same time.

I blink back the tears of confusion swirling in my head.

He looks wary, suspicious and frightened at the same time. He lets me see it all, and I am thankful. This is the most honest and open we have been with one another and it hasn't ended in an argument. I will take the victory.

I nod and a faint hint of a smile touches my lips. "Okay."

A line appears between his eyes. "Okay?"

"Yeah." I blow out a slow breath. "Did you tell me this before?"

His eyes shift around the room.

By now I know there's something he's hiding from me, something he's not telling me, but I allow it tonight because I can see how painful it is for him to bring up the small amount he told me.

"I did. And then your parents found out and wanted you to leave me. Said I wasn't good enough for you." He smiles sadly. "I can't say I blame them. I'm not. But I'm also smart enough to never want you to go."

"Is that why they don't like you?"

"Probably. I never cared too much about what they thought as long as it didn't change what you thought."

"Did it? I mean, I'm here, but yet, they won't even talk to me anymore."

Adam squeezes my hand and I turn to him so I'm facing him completely. His thumb lightly brushes over my knuckles, warming my skin and sending a different buzzing sensation through me.

"I think," he starts and rubs one hand through his hair. "I think they're more resigned than anything. They knew I wasn't leaving and they got tired of arguing with you about it."

I consider this and it only takes me a second to realize he's probably telling the truth.

The backing down doesn't sound much like my parents to me, but maybe my mom's way of refusing to return my recent calls and her silence at dinner is her way of punishing me. Like when she didn't talk to me about quitting dance.

"Come on," Adam says, and pulls me to my feet before I can dwell it for too long. "It's late and I didn't mean to drop this all in your lap tonight."

I follow him down the hall, stopping at my doorway before staring at the door to his room—our old room.

"Why did you, then?"

"Because you deserve the truth, and I don't want to lose you because I'm too afraid the truth will set your recovery further back."

I smile meekly. "Thank you."

And then I do something I don't have to think about. I take a step forward and gently press my lips against his. It's a quick kiss, and I barely feel his soft skin on mine before I step back.

"Um . . ." I say, and nervously play with the hem of my tank top. "Yeah. Good night."

Adam bites his bottom lip and smiles. There's a heat in his eyes and a playfulness in his look that says maybe he's relishing his own small victory of the night.

I duck into my room before I do something embarrassing like throw my arms around him just to feel his hard muscles against my skin again.

Unfortunately, I'm too restless to sleep. I lay in bed for hours, tossing and turning. Every time I close my eyes, I think of what Adam told me about his mom and his dad—about how he was raised—and somehow I understand the small things I know about him. I understand maybe why he sought love and attention from women, not caring how he treated girls. I understand his anger and the drinking.

It's all he's ever known. I see glimpses of a man that could mean he's trouble. Yet, I'm no longer afraid of him.

Not for my safety, anyway.

I just don't trust him. My head might, but my heart doesn't.

But for the first time, I truly *want* to.

He's opening up to me in a way that I can tell is difficult for him. I can see it in the tenseness of his shoulders and the tightness of his lips when he thinks about his dad or relives the things I remember. He hates that I've seen him like that.

And I hate that after a night of sharing what has to be difficult for him to talk about, I've left him alone.

I don't want him to be alone tonight and I'm tired of always feeling alone.

Before I can talk myself out of it, I'm in the hallway and opening the door to the room I used to share with him.

The only light is coming through the openings in the cheap, plastic vertical blinds by the window. I haven't stepped foot in this room since Adam brought me home from the hospital and I adamantly declared I wasn't sleeping in here. Not in this room with a stranger.

I take another step into the room, the floor creaking underneath my feet, and Adam turns in the bed, facing the doorway.

He props himself up on one elbow and then jumps out of the bed.

"Ames? What is it?"

I shift the weight on my feet, suddenly embarrassed and nervous that I'm even in here.

"Did you have a dream?" he asks, and reaches for my arms.

I tense under his touch.

"No," I say, my mouth and throat dry. I look into his eyes but all I see is the dark shadow of him in the room. I can't tell what he's thinking at all. "I was wondering if I could stay here."

His hands squeeze my arms and then relax. "Why? Are you sure you're okay?"

No, not really. I'm not. I don't know why I'm here. Why I have a sudden urge to hold him and be close to him.

"I don't want to be alone."

He exhales loudly and I can see the outline of his shoulders relax. He rests his forehead on mine and wraps me in his arms.

"Of course you can stay with me."

With my eyes closed, I let his deep and sleepy voice rumble over me, and my insides warm. I nod against him and move my arms so I can squeeze his hands.

He walks me to the empty side of the bed and pulls back the covers and then crawls into bed next to me.

"Can I hold you?" he asks, his voice as uncertain as I feel.

I turn over onto my side and let Adam lay down next to me, wrapping his arms around me, and pulling me to him.

"Thank you," he murmurs into my hair, squeezing me tightly, just as I finally drift to sleep.

~

"What in the fuck did you do to him?"

I jump back at the venom in Zander's voice. His anger pours out all over the place, filling the large entryway to the frat house. I've never seen his anger directed at me before. Hell, I've never seen anger like this from anyone before. Ever.

His piercings and tattooed arms that are crossed tightly over his chest scare the shit out of me.

"I . . . I don't know what you're talking about."

I jump at the sound of a loud crashing noise coming from upstairs and Zander glares at me.

"He's going ballistic and the only thing I can think to piss him off this much—is you. So tell me what in the hell happened last night." He leans forward into my personal space until I back up against a wall. "What did you do to him?"

"I didn't do anything!" I scream, and take off toward the stairway, taking them two at a time, scared out of my mind as to why Adam would be so upset.

He can't know that Brendan tried to kiss me again. I kneed him in the balls in the back hallway and there's no way Brendan would tell him unless he wanted to get his ass kicked.

Unless . . . unless Brendan claims I hit on him.

Shit. I wouldn't put it past him.

My body feels like it's on fire as I reach the top floor.

142

The sounds from behind the doorway are terrifying, and I jump as the sound of glass shattering reverberates into the hallway.

"Adam!" I yell at the same time I open his door. "What is . . ." My voice drops and hangs in midsentence when I survey the room in front of me.

The mirror over his dresser is cracked, pieces missing from it. The window to his room is shattered like he threw a chair—or a boulder—through it. Everything that sat on his dresser has been thrown to his floor and his smaller dresser has been knocked over.

The drawers have been thrown all over the room, and his clothes cover the nasty stained carpeting. There are holes in the drywall sprinkled all over the place. Holes that are clearly from him punching the wall.

"What did you do?" I ask, my voice hitching over my words when I finally find him breathing rapidly in a corner.

Blood drips from his hands and his shoulder. His chest is slick with sweat, and all he's wearing is a pair of gym shorts.

"What happened, Adam?" I ask, but stay in the doorway, too afraid to approach him.

He's completely trashed his room. Nothing is salvageable, except for maybe his bed.

He doesn't look at me. He says nothing.

He doesn't even move.

"If this is about Brendan, I can explain."

His head snaps to mine, and his eyes narrow. His nostrils flare and his hands tighten into fists. His chest raises and lowers and his cheeks are bright red.

"What do you mean, you can explain about Brendan?"

I shake my head, "Nothing, Adam. I just thought . . ." I look around the room. If I'm not the cause of his anger, then what in the hell happened to him?

"What in the fuck happened with Brendan!" He shouts so loud his voice vibrates off the walls in the room.

I hear footsteps coming from the stairway.

"Nothing! What did you do?" I shout equally as loud.

If being with Adam has taught me anything, it's that sometimes it's not only okay to yell, but it actually helps.

This time it doesn't.

"Get the hell out of here, Amy. I can't deal with this shit right now."

He stares out his broken window. I don't understand what's happening, but it's the first time in months I feel like we're miles apart. Misunderstandings and miscommunications pulling us apart from each other. Again.

He turns his eyes on me once more and bites out the words with such venomous anger, my eyes immediately fill with tears.

"Get. The. Hell. Away. From. Me."

"Adam."

"NOW!"

He roars, and I turn, running straight into Zander. He holds me with one arm, and shuts the door to Adam's room.

He doesn't look any more pleased with me than he did before.

"I didn't do anything," I choke out quietly over my tears and the thickness in my throat.

Slowly, Zander nods like he finally believes me, and his arm falls away.

I walk away, moving slowly down the stairs as another loud crashing sound echoes from Adam's room.

FIFTEEN

W̳hat made you come by yourself today, Amy?"

Dr. Jamison is wearing an ankle-length denim skirt and a lime-green T-shirt. It's the first time I've seen her match. Her hair is still braided, but she's wearing lip gloss, which is also new. I almost want to ask her if she has a date.

I chew on my bottom lip nervously, not sure where to begin.

"I had a rough dream last night."

"Did you ask Adam about it?"

"No, he yelled at me in it. His eyes looked so mad at me, and I obviously did something to make him mad." I lean back in my chair, closing my eyes, and remember the feral look in his angry eyes. "I just . . . I wanted to get your opinion on something other than my memories."

She scribbles something in a notebook and leans back in her chair. "Okay. What is it?"

"Is it possible for someone to grow up in an abusive home and not repeat the pattern?" I swallow the lump in my throat and squeeze my eyes shut. I almost feel like I'm betraying Adam by simply asking the question. And yet I haven't stopped wondering about it since I woke up from the dream, alone, in Adam's bed.

For the first time since I've seen Dr. Jamison, she stops smiling.

"What do you mean?"

"I just." I exhale slowly and try again. "In my dream, he destroyed his old room. I mean, he was really, really mad about something. He screamed at me and I left, but he's punched a wall in our hallway and he always seems so angry."

I roll my shoulders, trying to release the tension, but it doesn't help. My skin feels two sizes too small. "He told me his dad used to beat his mom; that his dad threw his mom down the stairs and Adam watched her die."

Tears fill my eyes immediately as I tell the story. They fall down my cheeks and drip from my chin before I can wipe them away. I reach next to the couch and blot my face with a tissue.

"Has Adam hurt you?"

I shake my head. "No, not that I know of, or remember anyway. But what if he has? What if he does and I just don't remember? What if . . . what if he hurt me?"

Dr. Jamison picks a nonexistent piece of lint off her skirt and leans back in her chair. She presses her lips together. My stomach rolls and then flip-flops again. I feel like I'm going to be sick, but I keep talking.

"He drinks a lot. Whenever he gets frustrated with me, the first thing he does is head to Zander's bar. He comes home drunk, punches holes in the walls, and destroys his furniture." I wipe my eyes again. I can taste the salt from tears in the back of my throat. "He scares me."

She nods, waiting for me to be done. I don't know what to do.

I believed Adam when he told me about his dad. I feel like I'm betraying him by being here, after he was so scared to tell me about his dad in the first place. He was worried it would put distance between us, but it didn't. For the night it brought us closer together, or at least I thought it did.

"Tell me something." I sniff through my tears and blink the rest away. "How does he make you feel?"

"What?"

"When you're with Adam. Tell me the first two things that come to your mind when you think of him."

"Confused and safe."

She smiles softly, knowingly. I frown.

How can I feel safe with him when I have so many questions?

"From what you've said, and from what I've observed, I don't think Adam has ever hurt you . . ."

"But does he have the ability to?" I interrupt.

She presses her lips together. "Maybe. But I've been doing this a long time, Amy. And there's a way that people in an abusive relationship interact with one another, even when they don't realize it. I don't think you and Adam have that relationship. Now, that doesn't mean you shouldn't be concerned. At the very least, perhaps you— or me—if you'd feel more comfortable, could suggest Adam take some anger management classes, or I could see him one-on-one as well. I could discuss his history with him privately and help him work through some of the things you said he's seen."

I consider it, at the very least, like she said. Maybe it'd help me feel better about being around him.

"I'd like that."

She leans forward and rests her hand on my knee. "If you don't feel comfortable with him, then the most important thing is to take care of yourself until you're ready. You've been through your own trauma and you still need to heal. Maybe there's somewhere you could stay until you feel better about being with Adam?"

I shrug. Not really, unless my parents are willing to have me move home again.

"I'll think about it."

I'm not sure how my car finds its way into my parents' driveway, but I'm here. I drove around Denver for hours after I left therapy.

Not ready to go home, not wanting to unload everything on Kelsey, and not feeling like spending the afternoon pouring over the books at Hooka Joe's either.

So here I am, my hands clenched around the steering wheel, in the curved driveway of the house I grew up in. An unfamiliar Acura SUV sits in front of me, and I stay in the car for who knows how long, debating whether or not to go in and interrupt whatever company my parents have.

Maybe Dr. Jamison is right. Adam and I just need some space.

Maybe some time apart will be good for me until I can remember what he's truly like without the stress of making him more upset or being uncomfortable in my own home.

Because my parents' home feels oh-so comfortable to me.

I snort, feeling ridiculous. I'm trading one jail for another. But it's for the best, I remind myself as I blow out a breath of air.

I'm just climbing out of my small BMW sedan when my parents' front door opens. I look over the top of my car and my mouth drops open.

My sister, Ann, looks at me wide-eyed and with a baby bouncing on her hip. My niece, Tilly.

I brace myself against my car door, hesitating to shut it. Maybe I should just leave. I can't believe my sister and her family are in town and my parents didn't even bother inviting me over to see them.

I shake my head in disgust. Some family I have.

"I didn't know you were coming," Ann says as she reaches the front of my car.

Her eyes flick back to the front door before returning to me. Tilly looks adorable. She has the slightest hint of my sister's blond hair and huge bright blue eyes. Coos and bubbles come out of her little mouth and then she squeals, throwing her arms in the air.

"Did Mom and Dad know you were coming?"

I reach out and hold Tilly's pudgy hand, still unbelieving that no one bothered to let me know my family was coming. My eyes burn with unshed tears, but I refuse to let them fall.

"No. I didn't know you were in town."

She frowns. "Mom said you didn't return her calls."

I scoff. "Mom never called me."

I can't take my eyes off my niece. She's at least four months old and I've never seen her. Without thinking, I reach out but pause right before I yank her from my sister's arms without permission. I look at Ann. "Can I?"

"Of course." She hands me Tilly and smiles. "I came out to get her diaper bag."

"Oh." I make a face and my sister laughs.

"Don't worry about it. I won't put you on diaper-changing duty yet."

I hold my niece awkwardly, still unable to understand why I've been cut off from my family. Why Mom hates me so much and why Ann has always been able to please her. I follow her back to the house, but when we hit the steps, she turns to me.

"Are you okay?"

"I don't know," I answer honestly. "Some memories are coming back, but there's a bunch of holes."

"I'm sorry I haven't been to visit you."

She looks like she means it. I don't know why she'd care. She's seven years older than me and we've never been more than two similar-looking girls who share a house together.

"No worries."

I follow her into the house, where it seems as if time stops as soon as we hit the kitchen. Ann's husband, Roger, is holding their son, Cooper. My mom and dad both turn to me, and my mom's face pales instantly.

She looks embarrassed that she just got caught in a lie. It pisses me off and my hold on Tilly tightens.

"So nice to be invited for dinner with the family."

My mom recovers and her mask of indifference and superiority is back in place in seconds. "I didn't think you'd show up."

"But you're my family."

My mom smiles, but it looks awkward on her perfectly made-up face. "You chose a new family. They can apparently give you something I never could."

She waves her hand in the air, as if I should be impressed with the marble floors, furniture so expensive that you're afraid to sit on it, and artwork that lines walls that are so beautiful but can't be touched unless you want to damage them.

"Carol," my dad scolds.

I throw up a hand and give Tilly back to Ann. "It's fine."

None of us move. Like we're not sure what to do with the red-headed stepchild that showed up uninvited. I suppose that'd be me. Uninvited to my home. Now where am I supposed to go?

I feel Ann pull on my hand and turn to face her. She's handed Tilly off to my dad and he's watching me, concerned, but not enough to stand up for me.

"Let's talk outside."

I follow my sister out because I know staying inside will only cause more arguments.

I sit next to her on the top of our cement steps and wrap my arms around my knees. I'm shaking, but I don't realize it until we're outside. My whole body is buzzing with adrenaline.

"I did come to see you," she says while I stare out at the fountain in the middle of our turn-around driveway. God, my house is pretentious. "When you were in the hospital."

"Why did you tell me before that you hadn't?"

She makes a face and looks away out to our perfectly manicured lawns. We actually have bushes that look like animals.

"I don't know. Because you weren't awake." She shrugs. "Because I didn't know if you'd even want me there."

"You're my sister."

A thick silence fills the small space between us. I don't even know what to say to her. How can my family be this screwed up?

"You were always the strong one, you know."

"What?" I ask, confused by the sudden subject change.

She smiles lightly. "Don't act like you don't know what I'm talking about. Ever since you were a kid, you fought against what Mom and Dad expected of you." She laughs, but it sounds sad. "I always admired that about you. Your ability to not care what she thought."

Adam's words from our trip to campus float through my mind. *They will always be disappointed with you.*

"And you?" I ask.

She releases a shaky breath. "I like my life. I always did. I really do love Roger, and I have two great kids."

"But?"

"But sometimes I wish I hadn't toed the line, had lived a little more before I followed the master plan and settled down."

"And I didn't toe the line?"

She snorts. "Please, Amy. You jumped the fence. Mom just doesn't know how to handle you."

"That's why she hates me?"

"She doesn't hate you. She just doesn't do well around people who are stronger than her."

I let those words seep into my bones. They warm me from the inside out. This may be the first real conversation I've ever had with my sister. And it sounds like she actually cares about me.

"Adam scares me," I tell her after another stretch of silence.

She nudges my shoulder, with a happier smile. "He is a bit rough around the edges."

"But?" I ask again.

She shakes her head. "I'd give anything to have Roger look at me the way I've seen Adam look at you."

I wrinkle my nose. "How's that?"

She wraps her arm around my shoulder. I'm not sure my sister has ever touched me like this except for the obligatory hug at family gatherings. I like it, and I sink into her embrace.

"Like he sees nothing else," she tells me, and smiles wistfully.

As if she's imagining what it would be like to be seen like that by someone.

SIXTEEN

"Where were you?" I bristle at Adam's rough tone when I walk through the door to our apartment.

It changes as soon as he sees my red, puffy eyes. I don't even know when I started crying, but I was wiping tears away on my drive home from my parents' house. I'm not sure why I'm so upset. Maybe it's emotional overload.

His hands are on my shoulders and he's looking at me intently. "What happened today?"

I push his hands away and walk to the kitchen.

I don't know how to begin explaining everything that went on today.

"I went to see Dr. Jamison today," I tell him, and reach for a bottled water in the fridge.

"I thought you said it was canceled?" he asks.

I shake my head and sit down on the couch. "I just had to talk to her about some stuff, and then I ended up at my parents' house."

He sits next to me. His lips are twisted into an odd shape and his eyebrows are pulled in.

I can feel confusion and concern radiating from him. I don't know how to begin to tell him about my dream last night or about what Dr. J. suggested or about my family.

That my sister actually cares about me. That might have been the strangest of all.

"How'd that go?" I look at Adam, his black hair wild from running his hands through it.

I shrug. "Did we ever go to my parents' house for dinner or anything and have it end well?" I know the answer based on his amused expression. "I talked to my sister, though. That was weird. Nice."

I shake my head and roll my water bottle back and forth in between my hands. "My sister and her family were in town and my mother didn't invite me to dinner, Adam. It hurts."

"What did she say to you?" His voice sounds strained, almost upset on my behalf.

I shake my head. "I don't want to talk about her anymore."

"Come here," he says, and pulls me to him.

He positions me so I'm tucked under his arm and my legs are draped across his lap. He holds me silently with one hand around my shoulders and his other hand resting on my hip.

It feels warm and comforting. He turns on a movie and just holds me.

I can't see the movie without turning my head, so I stay where I am, somehow feeling safe and protected even in the arms of a man who sometimes scares me.

And yet, like this, feeling his warmth all over, it's so easy to forget that. It's easy to lose myself underneath the feel of his muscles and his warm breath that whispers across my skin.

I'm barely paying attention to the laughter in the movie when Adam's thumb on my hips starts moving. I don't know if he's aware he's doing it or if he just can't help himself.

Slowly, I can tell his breathing has become heavier, slightly deeper, as the pad of his thumb finds the space on my skin just above my hip bone where my T-shirt has ridden up a little bit. The small warmth from his skin on mine sends pleasure throughout my entire body.

I don't think it's possible that I could physically react to him the way that I do if I was truly afraid of him. The realization shocks me and I tense in his arms.

His thumb stops moving and his hand moves away, but I stop him. "Don't."

I turn my face so my lips are inches from the skin on his neck. I don't know what kind of cologne he wears, and I don't care. All I know is that he smells absolutely delicious. But I'm terrified to make the first move again, scared he'll reject me and walk away all over again. That he won't be able to handle seeing my scarred skin.

"It felt nice."

I watch him swallow and his hand tightens on my hip, but still not where I want it. I want his hand back on my skin, warming me in a way that only he can seem to do.

I take a deep breath of my own and lean forward, brushing just a hint of a kiss on his skin. His breath hitches and his hand moves back to my waist, his full hand on my skin as he pushes up my shirt a little bit farther. His hand rests there, not moving at all, but even still, I shift underneath his touch.

It's a silent, but brave invitation, that I want more of him.

"You feel good," he whispers into my ear. I shiver underneath his husky rumbling. "You have no idea how amazing it felt to wake up this morning with you in our bed, curled up next to me." His tongue darts out and licks my earlobe, and then he presses a gentle kiss on the sensitive skin right behind my ear.

I moan softly into his neck. It comes out before I can stop it, and yet I'm not embarrassed or afraid of my response.

"Thank you for giving that to me." He pulls me close to him, shifting me so I'm straddling his lap, facing him.

I see lust and desire all over his face. And apprehension. Like maybe he's still afraid to push me too far. I wonder if my own expression mirrors his, because I feel the same way.

My hand moves to his chest and I feel his heart beating rapidly under my skin and his shirt. He looks down at my hand on him, then back to me. Both of his hands move to my hips and he rocks me once into him. My thighs tighten and relax and I stifle another moan as I feel his arousal underneath the crotch of his jeans. Hard. Wanting me.

I want it. I need it. I need something good to replace all of my fears.

Something to fill the emptiness that settles inside of me when I spend too much time alone, my mind wandering to all of the unknowns and holes in my memory.

Maybe I'm using him. Maybe I'm not. Maybe I truly want him and love him with all of my heart.

Right now, I just want to feel him. I want that connection with him.

One of his hands comes up and gently brushes my cheek, cupping it.

He pulls me closer so I'm inches from his lips. "I want to kiss you. And I don't want to stop."

My tongue licks my suddenly dry lips. "I want you to kiss me," I tell him, with a voice that must be mine, but I don't completely recognize. "And I don't want you to stop. Not tonight."

He studies me for a moment before he pulls me to him. Our lips join timidly at first, but he quickly takes control when he sucks my bottom lip into his and nips it lightly. I rock my hips into him involuntarily, and we both groan at the same time. My hands go to the back of his neck and I pull him to me, letting him know that I want this. That I'm not afraid of him.

"I need you, Amy. It's been too long," he tells me with a rough voice as he pulls away.

Without warning, he stands up, pulling me with him so my only option is to wrap my legs around his waist.

SEVENTEEN

He walks us to his room—our room—and places me gently on the bed. I have a feeling, based on the tension in his arms and the veins I can see protruding from his neck, that he's holding back and being gentler with me than he normally would.

And so I tell him. "You're holding back on me. Don't."

He shakes his head as he crawls over me, lifting my shirt and taking it with him as he moves closer to me. "I don't want to push you away. Not when I have you back in this bed."

I shake my head. "You won't."

He regards me for a moment, almost debating if my words are true. They are. At least for now. I only hope that I didn't just make a promise that I can't keep.

"God, you're beautiful," he tells me as he looks down over my body. I see him flinch when he gets to my scar, but I pull his face back to mine.

I see pain written all over him.

"You hate my scars."

He drops his head. "I hate that I didn't protect you."

I have no idea where my bravado comes from, but I lean forward and unclasp the back of my bra. The last thing I want is for him to leave me alone again, not when my entire body is coiled tightly with a sexual tension I never remember experiencing before.

His eyes watch every movement as I remove my bra and throw it onto the floor. I smile coyly.

"Then make it up to me."

He shakes his head, but he's smiling. It's such a rare thing to see on him, so I soak it all in, knowing I'm doing this to him.

I'm unraveling his self-control, and a part of me that I don't understand loves it.

He leans forward and kisses me. This time there's no gentle startup, no timidity or uncertainty. His mouth attacks mine like he's been starving for me. He drinks in every corner of my mouth like he owns me, possesses me. I move underneath him, shifting and pushing against him to relieve the tension that grows with every passing second.

Before I know it, my hands are on the back of his shirt, fisting it and pulling it off as fast as I can, but not nearly fast enough.

He breaks the kiss only to remove his shirt, and then his mouth is on my neck, his hands roaming and pressing all over my skin. His warm hands cup my breasts and he pushes them together, pulling them and massaging them. His fingers play with my nipples at the same time, bringing them to hardened peaks, and it sends a fire down to my lower stomach.

"Adam," I moan, and throw my head back. I need him. I need more of this.

His lips and tongue press against my skin as he moves down. His lips cover one of my breasts while his other hand continues kneading and teasing my other. I cry out, throwing my head back. I feel full of pressure. Full of something that is dying to be released.

"More," I moan, grinding against his crotch, needing the friction, but needing so much more at the same time.

My hands fight to get in the space between us and I'm unzipping his jeans and reaching into his boxers. Adam groans as I wrap my hand around his thickness.

He feels like the softest of silk over steel. I squeeze around him lightly and he bites on my nipples. I cry out again, rocking into him, and he pulls back away from me.

"You're killing me," he whispers and removes my hand from his jeans. "It's been too long."

"I need you."

Then, Adam's mouth is back on me, kissing my stomach while his hands work their way down to my jeans. He unzips them and leans back on his heels while he removes them and my underwear at the same time.

I resist the urge to cover up. To turn away from him. I can't.

His blatant stare on my body has me frozen to the bed with my hands fisting the covers beneath me.

"I need you, too." His voice is tight and rough. Deeper and full of unspoken tension that I'm just beginning to understand.

I take everything he gives me because my body feels like it's on fire with wanting him. In seconds, his jeans join mine on the floor and his hands and his lips are back onto my stomach, moving farther down. His warm hands spread my thighs and he stares at me.

"Beautiful," he murmurs against my skin as he begins pressing soft kisses against my lower stomach down to my thighs, avoiding all the areas where I need him.

My core pulses with need for him.

But he continues to tease me, gently licking me until I'm bucking my hips and moaning noises that sound animalistic to my ears.

He stops and pulls back, his hands firmly holding down my thighs. His eyes hold a fire that seems unquenchable. Do I always make him feel as out of control as he makes me feel?

"Do you want me?" he asks, with a wicked gleam in his eyes.

There's no way I could say no. Not now.

"Yes," I breathe out, trying to move against his hands that are holding me still.

"I need to hear you say it, Amy."

He leans forward as his hand cups me right where I want him. I move against him, not nearly gaining enough friction to do anything but aggravate me further.

His head lowers to my neck and he sucks my skin, biting it playfully and licking away the sting.

"I want you, Adam. Please."

I arch my back and turn my head, moving against his hand and lips just as he presses one finger, and then another, into me.

I moan and his mouth covers mine. His fingers press into me, sending me further into a vortex of emotions that feel ready to explode and shatter all over the place. His thumb presses against my clit, kneading it roughly as his fingers continue to pump back and forth with a firm rhythm.

And then I shatter.

My toes curl, my stomach tightens, my thighs press against the bed, and my back arches. I scream out Adam's name while he pulls back, watching me with a satisfied and lust-filled grin as I completely fall apart underneath him.

He pulls out every shudder of my orgasm with his fingers, and just when I think I can't take anymore, I feel the tip of his erection press into me. My body accepts him easily, greedily, still slick with moisture from my own orgasm. My hands fly to his lower back and pull him closer to me as his hips hit mine and he grinds into me.

"Uhh . . ." I moan, and bury my head into his neck, breathing his sweaty but sexy scent.

My lips press into his skin, tasting him and breathing him in. My body moves with Adam's as he rocks into me fiercely.

There is no slow passion with us. It's hard and rough and I feel myself being pushed across the bed with the force of his thrusts until my head is pressing against the headboard.

And still he doesn't stop. Thrusting into me powerfully as if it may be our last night. The only sounds that fill the room are of my blood beating in my ears, our skin slapping together, and both of our groans of pleasure.

"Amy . . ."

A new wave of pleasure grows inside of me just as Adam rolls us over.

I straddle him, clawing my hands into his shoulders and rocking my hips into him, pressing myself into another orgasm as Adam grabs my hips, moans loudly, and pushes into me. He pulls down on my hips at the same time and my clit rubs against his skin right where I need it to.

We explode together, moaning each other's names and shaking in pleasure.

I collapse on top of him and his arms wrap around me, holding me tightly to him. I can still feel him inside of me, emptying himself into me. Our hearts are racing against our sweat-lined skin.

We say nothing as we catch our breath.

"That was incredible," he whispers into my ear.

I mumble something unintelligible, unable to speak.

I close my eyes and rest against him, waiting for the voices of regret to begin speaking in my ear. Telling me that I just made a huge mistake, and yet, they're surprisingly silent.

All I hear is Adam's breath and all I feel is our hearts beating against our chests.

Slowly, he rolls us over to our sides and pulls out of me, taking care of the condom that I never noticed was put on, but am thankful he used anyway. When he returns to the bed, he brushes my dark, slightly sweaty hair off my cheek, and rests his hand at the base of my neck.

"What are you thinking?"

Nothing.

For the first time in the couple of months since I've woken from my coma, there is only silence in my head. There isn't the stress of trying to figure everything out or the doubt that I'm making the wrong choices. I'm completely relaxed.

I bite my lip.

He leans back, a frown line in between his eyes. I reach up with my thumb to smooth it out. "I think . . . that I might really like you."

His eyes light up and he pulls me closer, laughing softly against my neck. "I love you, Amy. You're my life."

I say nothing because I can't say what I know he wants me to. Hopefully the fact that I like him, and am willing to admit it, is enough for him tonight.

We rest against each other until I pull back and look at him. His dark eyes are half-closed and I know he's near sleep.

"I had a dream last night," I say softly, nervously.

He frowns again and I almost regret bringing it up.

"Was it bad?"

"You were really mad. You trashed your bedroom at the frat house. Zander yelled at me, and then you screamed at me when I mentioned Brendan."

"It scared you." It's a statement not a question. I shrug a shoulder, trying to play it off.

"I'm here talking to you about it instead of running away."

He rolls onto his back and throws an arm over his eyes, blocking me from being able to see him.

"My grandpa died. The one I went to live with after my dad . . ." He stops and I don't make him finish the thought. "My grandpa was a great guy," he says, rolling back to his side and resting a hand on my hip. He squeezes me playfully and I smile. "One morning, he just collapsed in his living room and died instantly."

"I'm sorry," I tell him, brushing my hand against his cheek and pushing his hair off his face. "You've lost everyone you cared about."

His jaw tightens and his eyes fill with tears, but I know he won't let them fall. His hands are tense on my body, and he presses his tongue against the back of his top teeth, regaining control.

"Almost." He chokes over the word, and I bury my head against his chest, wrapping my arms around him.

My own eyes fill with tears, but I'm not strong enough to blink them back or fight them away.

He means me.

I can feel it in the desperation of his voice, and I feel wrecked with emotion for this man who has seemed so scary to me.

Yet somehow I know he's freed me from an unemotional existence that was destined for me before he walked into my life.

I don't understand how. I don't remember when it happened, but I know it did because I'm not the girl I used to be.

And for the first time, I'm thankful to Adam for giving that to me. That gift of freedom and emotions and possibly the insanity I feel around him as well.

He had to have opened up something inside of me and now I just want to remember it all; all of my time with him, without the doubt of fearing him, too.

I pull him into my arms and we fall asleep, tangled in each other's arms and legs.

EIGHTEEN

"Here you go," I say, sliding Zander his black cup of coffee. His fingers tap mindlessly on the countertop and he doesn't take it right away. "Zander?"

"So you and Adam are doing better. At least that's what Kelsey says."

I nod, feeling slightly uncomfortable with the way he's looking at me. "Yes? I think so?" My voice trips and the words come out like questions instead of statements. "Why?"

"I just . . ." He stops, but his fingers keep drumming on the countertop. "I don't want to see him hurt by this. He has a lot going on."

My eyebrows pull in and I cock my head to the right. "What do you mean?"

"Nothing," he says, shaking his head. "Just . . . don't move forward until you know for certain you really want to be with him. Okay?"

"I'm not sure I'm following you, Zander."

"I know. But keep in mind what I said, all right?"

I shrug. Whatever. More cryptic language that isn't worth fussing over. "Okay. What's Kelsey doing today?"

He smiles, and I see a glint of his tongue ring flash in his mouth when he does it. "She's working. She'll be off around three." With that, he picks up his coffee and takes a quick sip. His lip ring clicks on the plastic top. "There's something else I wanted to talk to you about."

I raise my eyebrows, waiting for him to continue.

"I love Kelsey. A lot." His eyes dart nervously around the bar. I get the feeling that Zander might be less used to talking about his emotions or thoughts than even Adam is. "I asked her dad for permission to marry her."

My eyes fly open and I choke over absolutely nothing. Oh my gosh.

"You did? What'd he say?"

I try to picture Kelsey's dad, former quarterback to the Broncos, a big intimidating guy in his own right, and how he would handle Zander proposing to his daughter.

"He shook my hand and told me not to fuck up."

I laugh softly. "I could see that. Why are you telling me this?"

His nose wrinkles and he sets the coffee down on the countertop, but he leaves his hands on it like he needs something to do with them. "Other than her dad, you're the only person she cares about."

He looks at me knowingly, and it takes me a second to get what he's saying to me.

"You want my blessing?"

Zander bites the inside of his lip, and I think it's almost funny that he's so nervous talking to me about this. Hell, I don't even remember him. But that doesn't matter. I've known Kelsey long enough to know that if she's madly in love with someone, then he's perfect for her.

I walk out from behind the counter and throw my arms around him. He tenses and then he pats my shoulder awkwardly.

"I trust Kelsey to make her own decisions, Zander. If she chose you, then you're worth it. Congratulations."

"Yeah, well, she hasn't said yes yet."

"Any idea when you're going to ask her?" I ask, taking a few steps back.

He shakes his head. "Not yet. I don't want to fuck it up."

I laugh and the chiming bell of the door opening makes me move my eyes from him to the man walking into Hooka's. The man who somehow makes my heart skip a beat every time I see him.

I smile widely and pat Zander's shoulder. "You'll do fine. I'm happy for you two, really."

"Hey, beautiful," Adam says, and leans against the countertop when he reaches me. In the last couple of weeks since Adam and I first spent the night together making love, we've begun growing closer.

It's happened naturally, and I'm no longer sleeping in the guest room, but instead, I fall asleep every night curled in Adam's arms. My cheeks flush at the memory of making love to him this morning before he left for work.

Zander raises his cup of coffee and slaps Adam on the back. "I'm out of here. See you two around."

"What was he in here for?" Adam asks once Zander is gone.

"Coffee," I say with a smug grin. Adam catches it and smiles.

"He told you about proposing, didn't he?"

"Yup. He wanted my blessing."

"Did you give it to him?"

"Of course. Kelsey's smart."

I pour him his standard cup of Guatemalan brew and slide it to him.

"Do you have a break coming up?"

Hooka's is currently packed. I've been on my feet for hours serving customers left and right, but fortunately, there are no customers in line and everyone at the tables seems content.

"What's up?" I walk out from behind the counter and follow him to the worn leather chairs by the fireplace.

"I have to go out of town for a few days."

He licks his lips and blows on his coffee, cooling it. It reminds me of how his tongue was all over my skin just a few hours ago and suddenly sitting by the hot fireplace feels like I just got thrown into a furnace.

"Amy?" he asks, a weird look on his face.

"Um . . . yeah. Sorry. What were you saying?"

"I need to go out of town for three days. For work."

I frown. "For what? You work for a local developer."

His mouth twists into a funny shape. He's lying to me. I don't know how I know. I just know he is.

My eyes widen as I watch him silently rehearse his excuse.

"It's some conference in New Mexico. A boring thing about using more ecological sustainable materials."

"Right."

I purse my lips and nod my head because that's what he expects me to do, but I know he's lying. I just can't figure out why he would do this. Why now when things are—were—going so well with us?

I stand up and brush the invisible crumbs off my black apron. "Okay, then. When do you go?"

"Tonight. I'll be back Friday."

I want to call him on it. I'm not stupid and it's offensive that he thinks I'd believe this. There's no way he has to attend a conference ten hours away and he's just now hearing about it.

But instead of bringing it up at work, I let it go.

"All right, then." I press my lips together. "Anything else you want?"

He frowns and takes a step closer to me. "Are you okay?"

Are we okay is the question he's really asking. I'm not sure what to tell him. Two weeks of trust after months of confusion is being flushed down the drain right in front of me.

"You bet. I need to get back to work." He sighs and nods, like he understands. I know he's lying. He knows I know. And yet, neither of us says anything. "See you Friday, then."

I turn around and he holds my wrist, pulling me back. He stares at my lips like he wants to kiss me, but I take a step back, not allowing it.

"I'm at work, Adam."

"All right. I love you."

I nod once.

It doesn't sound like he loves me, not right now. It sounds like one of those obligatory sayings the couple that has been married for forty years has said every day, twice a day. There's absolutely no emotion and no conviction behind the words.

Three empty words hang between us and I leave them there, disappearing into thin air as I turn my back on Adam and pretend I have work to do in the office.

And then something stops me.

I'm not that girl who puts up with people lying to my face. I've fought too hard to get to a place with Adam where I'm beginning to feel something real for him, something that may be different from what we had before, but it's there.

I feel it when he pulls me into his arms and when he throws that sexy crooked grin in my direction.

I follow him outside.

He's just a few feet ahead of me when I call his name and he turns around.

He runs his hand through his hair and takes a couple of steps in my direction. I fidget with my hands, unable to decide if I should cross my chest and protect myself or put them on my hips defensively. In the end, they fall lamely to my sides.

"Why are you lying to me?"

His chin jerks, shocked either by my bluntness or my ability to read him.

"What is it?" I ask, feeling a nervous energy flood my body. Maybe I don't want the answer to what he doesn't want to tell me.

He exhales a deep breath and reaches for me. I pull away and decide to cross my arms after all.

"My dad has a parole hearing tomorrow. I have to be there."

Nervousness floods his face although I don't understand why. My heartbeat doubles as I consider what this means to him. I know so little of what he's told me about his dad and his mom. But my heart breaks for him.

To have to see his dad in prison, knowing what he did.

Knowing that Adam had to see it. Forced to watch his mom die.

"I don't know what to say."

He reaches for my hand, pulling me closer to him. This time I let him. I want to comfort him. Pull him into my arms and pull his face down to the crook of my neck and hold him tightly, but I can't.

He was going to Iowa to go through this. Alone. And he lied about it.

I no longer understand my role with him. Who I am to him.

"I just found out," he sighs again, and grasps my hand tighter. "I'm sorry."

For lying or for hiding it? I don't have the confidence to ask.

I fidget back and forth on my feet, completely unaware of the street traffic passing us by or that I've left Hooka's completely unattended. I don't know if any customers have gone in while I've been outside.

I'm searching for something in Adam's eyes. Something to bring me comfort or assurance, but there's just a dull blankness in them. He's hiding from me.

"Would you have told me?"

He lets go of my hand like it burned him. His hands return to the back of his neck and clasp together. "I didn't think you were ready."

I pull back like I've been slapped. Angry that he gets to decide what I'm ready for. Hurt that he doesn't trust me enough to be honest with me.

"Ready for what? The truth? To be there for you?" I'm pissed as my tirade begins but am unable to stop it. "Would you have told me before all of this?"

"Yes!" His hands slam against his sides and they tighten into fists. "We didn't hide things from each other. Not like this. Of course I would have told you."

"But not now. Why?"

"Because no matter what you say, I still see the hesitancy in you when I come too close. The times that I touch you and you flinch."

"I don't."

"You do."

As if to prove his point, he reaches for me. My right shoulder immediately jerks back.

I'd like to tell him it's because I'm pissed and angry and hurt but even I know it's a lie. It's a small jerk, almost unnoticeable to me. But Adam has seen it before. Enough to know.

"You do, Amy," he repeats, and pulls me to him.

His hand reaches around and clasps the back of my neck, pulling my face so it rests against his chest. I go willingly this time. Ashamed that I could think things were going so well but clearly they aren't. Will I ever trust him fully?

"I'm not upset. I get it, I do. I just . . . I can't put you through a parole hearing with my dad. I can't have you see him and wonder if I'm like him."

"I wouldn't."

"You would." Regret laces his voice as his warm lips brush against my temple and down my jaw. "It's hard enough to bear when we're alone. I don't think I could handle seeing fear on your face with that monster in the same room."

"You're not him." I know he's not. Tears fall down my cheeks and I turn my head so I don't get his shirt wet. Guilt consumes me that I've made him feel like this.

"I need to go, and I need to do this."

"I want to be there for you."

"You can be," he whispers against my skin and pulls me in for a kiss. It's warm and hot and makes my knees turn to jelly instantly. "When I get back, okay?"

I nod, although I don't fully understand.

"I love you." There's more conviction this time, but the emotion is still lacking. I try to tell myself it's because of his dad. That it has nothing to do with me. But I can't make myself believe it. "I'm sorry I lied about it."

I sniff the remaining tears away and wipe my cheeks.

"I get it." Even though I don't. I look into Hooka's, remembering where I am finally. "I'll see you soon?"

"Three days."

I walk inside, leaving him on the sidewalk because I'm not sure what else to say. What can I do to soothe him and make him believe that seeing his dad, hearing the testimonies of how he killed Adam's mom, wouldn't scare me? I'd be lying just like Adam did to me.

By the time I get home, the apartment is silent and I know that he's already gone.

I decide I have two options. I can be "that girl" and run down to the corner grocery store and grab a quart of Cherry Garcia ice cream and wallow for a few hours.

Or I can drink.

◈

"Drink!" I slam my hand down at the bar and wave for Zander to slide another shot my way. He looks at Kelsey for approval, who nods.

"How's work going?" I ask her.

She's a nurse on the oncology floor. It has to suck. I've never been able to handle being around dying people. They make me nervous.

"Long and exhausting," she tells me as we take a sip of our beers. "I have two patients who aren't doing so well right now."

She shakes her head, erasing the memories of her day. I don't blame her. It'd be impossible to not bring that sort of work home with you. Thank goodness I'm just a manager at a coffee bar.

"So what are you going to do when Adam comes back?"

I frown into my empty shot glass and slide it toward the edge of the bar so Zander can give me another. She just brought up the elephant in the room that I've been trying to avoid.

"Not sure. I figure I have two options," I say, and hold up one finger. "I can be pissed he lied to me and tried to keep something important from me." I flick up a second finger and nod a thank you to Zander for the new shot. "Or I can realize that our relationship is just as he said—not where it used to be."

The liquor catches over a lump in my throat at my own disappointment in realizing that.

Kelsey smiles widely and wiggles her eyebrows. "That makes you upset."

I hate that being friends with someone forever means that they can read you better than you can read yourself sometimes. And I hate that she seems thrilled at my disappointment.

"It means that, regardless of everything else, I care about him."

"You lo-ove him," she sings, and it's clear we've had too many shots as she covers her mouth and giggles.

I blink and shake my head. "No. But lately, I guess I've seen glimpses of why I once did. And maybe I'm not as scared of him as I thought I was."

I stare awkwardly at the shot glass in my hand and wonder if Zander put a special truth serum in it.

I'm not afraid of Adam.

I roll the thought around in my head for a bit while Kelsey smiles at me softly.

I am not afraid of Adam. I'm not. I know it with certainty.

And with the realization, I feel a weight leave my shoulders that I didn't know was there. I graciously take the bottle of beer Zander put down without me having to ask. He nods his head in my direction and watches me, expecting something.

"So what's holding you back, then?" Kelsey asks, breaking through the fog in my head.

"I don't know." I shrug and pick at the paper label on the bottle.

My tongue feels heavier than it should and my cheeks feel warm. I've clearly had too much to drink, I think, and push the beer away from me.

"Maybe it's just the not knowing."

"Not knowing what?"

I look over her shoulder at the crowd behind her. It's Tuesday night and the tables aren't completely full, but there's a small group of guys in the back playing pool. Slapping each other on the backs with easy smiles on their faces. A girl is standing in between the knees of a guy sitting on a barstool. One of his hands holds a cue stick, the other a beer bottle, and both hands rest on the girl's hips as she smiles at the man she clearly loves.

He throws his head back and laughs, placing a kiss on her forehead before he gets up and goes to take his shot.

"Not knowing what it was like to fall in love with him in the first place."

I turn back to Kelsey, whose lips are puckered in thought.

"I think we should go to the cliffs tomorrow."

I frown, confused by the subject change.

"It'll be fun," she says, and claps her hands. "We can take lunch and walk off the hangovers we're totally going to have. Where else have you ever gone that makes you feel more peaceful and helps you think more clearly?"

"Kelsey, I'm not sure that's a good idea."

I turn to Zander's deep voice from his side of the bar.

"Why not?" I ask.

He looks between the both of us, uncertain and maybe annoyed. Like going to the cliffs is wrong.

"Because you're not healed enough to walk that far."

Even he doesn't believe his own excuse. My casts have been off for weeks and it's only a three-mile walk once we park the car.

"She'll be fine," Kelsey says, like she just scolded a child.

He shakes his head, but it makes me more determined to go.

"Sounds perfect," I say with a smile.

NINETEEN

Y ou're acting weird," I tell Kelsey as I watch her fidget with her fingers.

She's been quieter than normal ever since she took me to my apartment this morning after I passed out on her couch last night. She waited while I showered and got dressed for a hike. My head has been pounding from the excessive liquor we overly filled our stomachs with. Even my sunglasses aren't helping my eyes from feeling like they're getting stabbed with toothpicks from the harsh sunlight.

Hangovers suck.

"My head hurts," she moans, and I almost believe her. But then she bites her thumbnail absentmindedly and I know she's hiding something.

I shrug and follow her as she veers off to the last path that we have to take to get to my favorite cliffs. It's so narrow you have to walk through it single file and it weaves around the natural evergreens that fill the mountains. It's barely a path, mostly just worndown ground from the few hikers like us who like to go off the main trails and explore the woods on our own.

Kelsey and I found this area when we were sixteen. It's always been our escape. Our safe haven.

I take a deep breath as we cut through the last of the trees into the open area. The air is crisp and clean and cool, even though it's the height of summer. But we're so high up we have our fleece jackets on to keep us warm.

Across from my favorite cliffs, there is an area that looks like a bomb exploded. It opens into a wide, circular, and jagged expanse that ends at least twenty-five feet below us, but has one large opening directly in the center that produces a gorgeous waterfall.

I smile as I remember all the guys Kelsey and I used to be friends with in high school. They loved trying to prove how manly they were by jumping off the cliffs, landing in the warm water below.

Kelsey and I were never dumb enough—or brave enough—to follow their lead.

I don't realize that I've stopped at the edge of the clearing, the sounds of the rushing water from the waterfall so familiar it's like my own heartbeat, until Kelsey makes a pained noise and squeezes my hand.

I look at my hand that she's squeezing tightly and then at the edge of the cliffs.

They're destroyed.

Our favorite place looks as if it's been washed away into the oblivion below. The lush green grass and rocky edge now looks like a melted puddle of mud. The edge of the cliffs are at least twenty feet closer to us than they should be.

"Oh no," I whisper, saddened that my favorite place to go in the entire world is just . . . gone.

I look at Kelsey. Her eyes carry a sad expression, and she releases my hand, rubbing her own two together.

I take a few steps forward, sadness and apprehension rippling through me. "What happened?" I ask Kelsey. My question is met with silence, and I turn back to her. She's watching me curiously.

And then her face puckers into something unreadable.

"This is where you were hurt."

"What?" My head snaps back to the edge.

It had to have been a mudslide. It's the only thing that makes sense, and they aren't uncommon during the spring in the mountains with the melting snow and rain showers.

I'm staring at the destruction, walking closer, as if pulled to the edge to see exactly what happened to me. A sick feeling rolls through me and I stop.

And I hear him.

Adam.

"I've never loved anyone the way I love you, Amy. I never wanted to love anyone."

My eyes dart around. I spin to the trees, turning in a slow circle, as if I expect him to appear directly in front of me in the sunshine.

I frown. He's not even here. He's in Iowa. I know this, and yet suddenly I feel as if he's right next to me and holding my hand, which feels too warm to not be enclosed in someone else's.

I look down at my left hand. I turn it upside down and, moving it in small circles, fisting it and relaxing it, wonder where the heat is coming from when it shouldn't feel any different than any other part of me.

I look back at Kelsey, but she's several feet away from me.

"What happened?" I ask. My throat is tight and my words are scratchy. Tripping over themselves as they work their way out of my mouth.

Her lips pull into a tight line and I see tears form in her eyes. She shrugs one shoulder, looking out over the waterfall, and says nothing.

I turn back around slowly, my eyes still scanning the area. All the answers I've been wanting, been trying so hard to bring to the front of my mind, are here in this very place.

I can feel it.

And slowly, they begin to come to me in colorless images like picture snapshots until everything is lined up exactly the way it is supposed to be.

I look back down at my hand and hold it with my right hand as my knees hit the dirt below me. And the first tear rolls down my cheek.

∾

"I've never loved anyone the way I love you, Amy. I never wanted to love anyone." Adam takes my hand in both of his, kissing each knuckle. His lips turn into a nervous smile right before he drops to a knee.

My eyes flash open. I open my mouth and then close it. Wanting to say something but not knowing what to say.

"We're still young. I know we are. And I know we're just getting our lives started, but I want to do it together. You and me—forever."

"Adam . . ." His name comes out choked through tears. Emotion overcomes every single one of my senses. I stare at him through wet eyes. Never would I have thought this is what our picnic today was for.

"Marry me, Amy. Marry me and be with me forever."

I don't hesitate. I don't have to. I've known Adam is the only man I'm going to love ever since I finally decided to give him a chance and go on the date he fought so hard to get.

"Of course I'll marry you."

He doesn't say anything as he slides the small platinum band and solitaire diamond on my finger. I don't care that it's small. It's from Adam and the only thing I care about is being with him forever.

He pulls me to him, and I fall down, pushing him onto the ground that's still wet from the snow and the early morning rain. It almost ruined our day trip, but I'm so glad the sun is shining now, warming the ground and the air.

I kiss him without hesitating. Our lips hit together in a passion that is unexplainable. And unavoidable.

I should know.

I tried as hard as I could to avoid the emotions that awakened in me just being near this man.

But the fight was useless. I was always going to belong to him.

Adam wraps his hands around my waist as he holds me to his chest; my cheeks are wet from my tears. Laughter escapes both of us, even though our lips are still connected.

He pushes forward so he's sitting straight up and I wrap my legs around him.

"There's one more thing we need to do today," he says to me, brushing back my hair from my face. It's stuck to my cheeks and neck from the wetness of my tears.

"Another surprise?" I ask, baffled.

I look between his eyes that have never shown so much happiness in them and down to my ring. It may be a small diamond, but it sparkles as bright as the sun.

"We're jumping. You and me, Amy. Fighting our fears together."

My eyes widen and my heart skips a beat. Or twelve.

"Adam," I say warily.

He holds up a hand to stop me. Then he stands up, still carrying me wrapped around him.

"We can do this. It's just like anything else we've fought for in order to be together. You're brave enough for this."

He walks me to the edge and sets me to my feet. My legs are shaking and he holds my hand, squeezing tightly.

"You've always wanted to do this," he says to me, looking at me and then to the water below us.

"It's going to be freezing." I shake my head and take a hesitant step backward, back to the safety of the grass and our Broncos picnic blanket.

But he doesn't let go of me. He holds my hand firmly and pulls me back to him.

I chew nervously on the inside of my lip as he looks down at me, brave enough for the both of us. Always willing to fight for us. For me. Even when the easy thing to do would have been to just walk away.

But that's not Adam. He's a fighter.

He's fought for everything he has, and I know by looking at the brightness in his eyes that he will fight for this, too. For me to conquer the last fear I have.

And I won't let him down. Not when I've struggled so much to get to where I am. Independent and strong on my own two feet. I now know exactly what I want for my life, and I've done it all by mapping out my own plan with Adam's encouragement and support.

He smiles when he sees my determination to follow him. Jumping blindly into the air all because I know he'll be there to catch me at the bottom.

"On the count of ten."

I shake my head quickly. "Five."

I need a smaller number so I don't have the time to change my mind. He laughs softly and brushes a light kiss across my lips.

"I'm going to love you forever, you know."

"Me too." I smile and press my lips against his, firmly.

I squeeze his hand as we stand at the edge.

I take a deep breath as he says the word five. My feet shake and I hear a soft rumble in my ears.

"Four."

My heart lodges in my throat and my knees bang together. I feel one light raindrop on my nose and I look to Adam.

He smiles. "Three."

My feet shake again and I hear a cracking sound. Adam squeezes my hand tighter and I feel a slight tug in it.

His eyes flash with worry, but I'm too concerned about the jump to stop and question him.

"Amy," he says, and tugs me harder.

The ground rumbles beneath my feet again and it suddenly hits me that the shaking isn't from nerves.

I take a step toward Adam, my eyes widening as I move.

"Adam."

And then my feet slip, yanking me out of Adam's hand.

"ADAM!" I shout, right before the mud covers me and everything goes black.

TWENTY

I'm gasping for breath. My hands are digging into the dirt underneath my fingertips, but I can't say anything. I can't see anything.

All I can feel is my body heaving everything out of my stomach that I've eaten in the last twenty-four hours.

"Amy."

Kelsey's voice barely breaks through the ringing in my ears as I continue heaving the remainders of my breakfast and last night's tequila and beer onto the ground below me.

"Oh my God," I gasp through strangled tears and emotions that clamp down on my throat like a vise.

I survived a mudslide.

I squeeze my eyes shut, willing the images I suddenly see so clearly to disappear into oblivion.

I don't want this memory. Not the one that shows how I could have died. How I should have died.

My right hand moves to my abdomen, where my fingers run along the jagged scar, the one that sliced me open from breast to hip. I shake my head to get rid of the sight I can now see replaying through my mind.

Everything.

It hits my mind like the avalanche that Dr. Hassen warned me about. I press the sides of my head with my dirty fingers as the tears fall down my face, only vaguely aware that Kelsey is calling my name and shaking my shoulders.

◟

"Look at that," Adam's crooked grin is contagious. I smile as I see the bright red A on his statistics test right before he slams it down on my desk.

He stands above me, leans down, and whispers in my ear, "You owe me that date now."

"You don't date," I remind him of what he said to me last week in the library.

Inside, my heart is fluttering madly out of control. I thought he'd get over this mad obsession with taking me out on a date weeks ago.

He wiggles his eyebrows once. "You promised. A deal's a deal."

I feign a scowl. I really do want to go on a date with him. "Fine. One date."

"We'll see." He bends down and grabs my backpack, throwing it over his shoulder.

The move baffles me, yet I'm turned on by the confidence he carries himself with. How can anyone be so sure of themselves? Most of the time I feel like I'm floundering in a fishbowl, wanting to break out of the bowl but getting nowhere. Just peering out and seeing everyone else living the lives they *want to have.*

"Today," he says, grinning.

I scoff. "It's Tuesday."

"People don't date on Tuesdays?"

I laugh and notice that his hand is on the small of my back, leading me out into the quad where hundreds of students will see me with Adam Taylor. Instantly, I move away from him and turn around, reaching for my backpack.

"Fine. What time?" I ask, trying to hide my excitement.

Fine, I want to go on a date with Adam. It's not like I haven't heard the constant rumors about him. How hot he is, how good he is in bed, and even though that last one makes me nervous given my inexperience, it doesn't mean it's not tempting.

"After class."

"A day date? You really don't know how to do this, do you?"

He throws his head back and laughs before his eyes meet mine. He sobers immediately, taking the two steps in between us and closing the gap.

His lips brush against my cheek. I gasp at the warmth and the softness of them. They're gone before I even knew they were there, but my entire body feels like it just went up in flames.

"You'll want more than just an hour or two with me."

I stand there, frozen, as he heads out the door and high-fives his teammate and best friend, Zander, out on the front lawn.

∽

"Amy!" I jerk back from the forceful push and gasp. Kelsey is instantly in my face. "What in the hell is happening to you? We need to go!" She's pulling my hand, forcing me to my feet before I can answer her, and I trip over my feet, almost falling back into the dirt.

"I saw it," I gasp, still trying to catch my breath and erase the flood of memories that simply won't stop.

"I figured. We need to get you home."

I squeeze her hand, not saying anything. I focus on the steps on the narrow lane, and for the forty-five-minute trip back to my apartment, I sit in her Camry, shaking, and remembering everything.

∽

"I'm really sorry about dinner tonight. I didn't think it would be that bad."

Adam wraps his arm around me and pulls me to him, dropping a soft kiss on my temple.

I shrug. "Okay, so I knew it was going to be really bad. But God." I drop my head into my hands that are propped on the table at Martino's. "My mom is such a bitch. I'm so sorry I subjected you to her line of bullshit."

Adam's warm hand rubs my back and he leans in, pressing a quick kiss against the skin on my neck. "I don't give a shit what your mom says about me, Amy. We both knew she wasn't going to like me and it's not like we tried to impress her or anything tonight."

I shake my head and start laughing. I can't help it.

What in the hell was I thinking, showing up for Thanksgiving dinner with my entire family, bringing Adam for the first time, and we're both wearing jeans? And me in a faded gray vintage-looking T-shirt from an indie rock band we went and saw last week. I'm lucky my mom's head didn't explode all over the Thanksgiving turkey.

"I totally screwed this up," I groan.

I should have known that breaking out from my parents' protective and obsessive watch would blow up in my face.

"What do you want me to do? Because I'll do it. We can go find a suit and then dress you up like their little doll if you want to head back and salvage this dinner. I don't really care. I just want you to be happy."

I shake my head. "They have to accept it at some time. Might as well be today."

"Okay . . . so what do you want?"

I lean back in the booth, my head resting on the top of the leather padded seats and my eyes catch sight of my favorite wind chime. They're butterflies. Silver and so frail it amazes me that they haven't broken yet. It seems like just the smallest gust of air would splinter the frail wires.

"I want to be free."

Adam reaches over and grabs my hand, squeezing it tightly. His other thumb brushes away the tears running slowly down my cheeks. His touch is protective and loving, just like always.

"Then that's what you'll be."

~

"What in the hell was that shit?"

Adam's booming voice makes me pause in the parking lot. My heart is still beating out of control. I think I might have a stroke.

I feel Brendan tug on my hand toward his truck, but I stop.

What am I doing? Even if Adam just made out with Britnee, Brendan is the biggest douche in the entire world.

Adam makes me lose my mind. I no longer know if this is a good thing or the worst possible thing to happen in the entire world.

My precise life, neatly organized into its perfect little boxes, shattered the moment Adam's lips first met mine.

"Stop! Damn it, Amy!" His hand grabs mine, pulling me so tightly that my hand is ripped out of Brendan's grasp.

"Hey," he protests. Adam levels him with a look.

"Go back to your date, Whitaker."

Brendan puffs out his chest. Oh shit, a pissing contest. Fabulous. Just what turns me on.

I put my hand on Brendan's chest, stopping him from moving. "I shouldn't have done that. I'm sorry. But there's no way in hell I'm going home with you."

He shrugs and gives me a lopsided, cocky smile. Damn. I really do hate him. "It's not like you'd be that good anyway. Everyone at the house knows you're just a lame piece of pussy—"

The next thing I know, Brendan's head flies back and he's on his back in the parking lot, holding his nose, covered in blood and moaning.

"Say it again, you fucker!" Adam yells, bending over him, his breath panting.

"Adam." I reach out for his hand. Maybe he's just as insane with the thought of someone touching me as I am about someone—Britnee especially—getting their hands on him. We're such a wreck.

But it's the most glorious wreck I've ever seen.

He looks at me, his hands fisting and releasing.

"You were seriously going to go home and fuck him? Just because Britnee threw herself at me?"

I run my hands through my hair, disgusted this night that was going to be so perfect has taken such a shit-tastic turn.

"I don't know! I was just . . . pissed! I planned on us being together, and you're you—and I'm me—and I saw Britnee's hands all over you and I just freaked out!" My hands wave madly in the air. I feel like a lunatic, and I'm sure I don't look sane.

"'You're you—and I'm me'—what does that mean?" He takes a step over Brendan. Adam's foot pushes him back to the ground and he moans again. Then Adam takes my hand and pulls me away.

"You're . . . magnificent," I mutter, and blush heatedly. Thank God it's dark out here and he can't see me. "From what I hear anyway. And I couldn't . . ." I pull my eyes to him, letting him see my vulnerability for the first time. "I couldn't even keep Tyler happy."

Adam laughs. He laughs so hard that I start to get pissed.

"Hey!" I yell, slapping him against his chest.

"You are such a girl. This is about sex? You're freaking out because you think you won't be good in bed?"

I bite my lip and look away.

Adam laughs harder. He's not helping my ego. I open my mouth to tell him, but I don't get a word out.

His mouth hits mine, his hands cup my cheeks, and I gasp into his mouth. His body molds to mine, and he walks me backward until I bump into a car. It's not his, and I don't care if the owner sees us defiling it. Adam's lips on mine erase every thought, every insecurity, I've ever had.

"We're going. Now. And we're going to the Lux, and I'm going to prove to you exactly how happy you'll make me."

He tugs my hand again, leading me like he always does, muttering under his breath. "All this dramatic shit for no reason. I swear to

God, Amy. If you don't know how fucking crazy I am about you after tonight, then I'm spending the rest of the weekend proving it to you."

I gulp. An entire weekend of sex with Adam? He might break me.

∼

"What is this?" Adam asks, a smile on his face from ear to ear.

I blush. I look at him, waving my photos in the air. "It's my box."

He laughs that laugh that heats my insides. "I thought you were unpacking the apartment today."

I look around our room in our tiny little apartment. I love it. It's my favorite place in the world, even if it is a disaster. Boxes are opened in every available space and we have yet to set the beds up. We still haven't bought furniture, but we're supposed to go tonight.

"I got sidetracked," I tell him, and give him a kiss when he leans closer, still grinning. "Look at these."

I show him the photo of the day his frat house had a car wash in a grocery store parking lot in downtown Denver. Adam laughs into my neck when he sees the photo of him and me wearing matching bikinis.

All the guys wore bikinis that day for extra attention. Kelsey and I helped pick out bikinis for Zander and Adam, and then later, we went back and bought matching ones in our sizes.

Adam's cradling me in his arms and we're both soaking wet. It was right after Kelsey hosed me down with the water and I almost slipped on the pavement.

"I love you," I tell him, and kiss him again. His lips press harder against me, his hand brushes down the side of my cheek, and he leans me back onto the floor, climbing on top of me.

"I will love you forever."

"You better. Not like you can get better." My laugh turns into a

gasp as soon as Adam leans down, nips at my collarbone, and rocks his pelvis into me.

~

"Amy?" Kelsey's voice cuts through the haze, and I open my eyes. We're sitting in my apartment building parking lot.

I suddenly don't want to go in, knowing it's empty and knowing the reason is because Adam didn't trust me to not run from him when I heard what his dad did to his mom. Shame fills me and it might be unwarranted, but I have to make this right.

"I called Zander," Kelsey says, and unbuckles. "I told him I plan on staying here tonight. You don't need to be alone right now."

I nod and then frown. I was so out of it I didn't even hear her on the phone in the car? I blow out a breath, overwhelmed, and get out of the car.

She follows me into the apartment, and once inside, I head directly to my closet. The one Adam and I shared.

I hear Kelsey's footsteps following me. I don't stop to look at her. I feel possessed. On a mission to see the truth confirmed. How happy Adam and I were. How much he loved me.

How much I loved him.

I dig through the closet, laughing silently that empty shoeboxes cover the floor and are stacked four boxes high.

When I find the one I saw in my memory, I pull it out, sinking down to my knees, resting my butt on my heels. My fingers hover over the top.

Kelsey puts a hand on my thigh and nudges her shoulder into mine. "Open it."

I turn to her and give her a shaky smile. She nods and I do what she said.

I gasp.

Inside, the box is jam-packed with hundreds, if not thousands, of photos.

But the sheer enormity of my obsession of printing out photos in the day of digital technology doesn't faze me.

The pale blue box sitting right on top does.

My hands fly to my mouth as if I am again seeing him ask me for the very first time. Tears drip down my cheeks and I feel Kelsey's arms wrap around me.

"You remember," she says softly. Happily.

"Everything." I sniff and reach out for the box. I hold it. Wanting to open it but nervous. It's not mine to have yet, not until Adam gives it to me. I bite the edge of my bottom lip, wiping my eyes, and smile at Kelsey.

"I need your help."

～

Kelsey makes the phone calls, after I hand over my credit card, while I throw some clothes in a carry-on.

Adam may not have wanted me to be there for him, but that was before.

Now I want to be there to support him. He needs me and I'm committed to doing that, because I now know he was always there for me.

I throw the bag over my shoulder and head out to the kitchen, where I hear Kelsey talking on the phone with Zander. He's going to try to see if he can figure out where the parole hearing is.

I take the corner into our kitchen too sharply and my hip slams into the green, retro-looking metal table.

～

"This couch is perfect."

Adam scowls, but his eyes are laughing at me. I look around the consignment store.

"It's stained and looks like a rat died in it."

"Exactly. We'll never care if we get it dirty. Oh look! A coffee table with water rings," I say, clapping my hands. "Perfect!"

"You're being really weird."

"I never had this stuff. Things that felt like a home instead of a museum. Just let me, please?" I ask, fisting his shirt in my hands. I try to pout but fail miserably.

Adam laughs and pulls me to him. "You're insane and I love you. If you want shitty furniture, shitty furniture is what you'll get."

"Yes!" I do a fist pump, dancing around the smelly and dusty consignment store while I pick out other completely mismatched pieces for our apartment.

～

I blink and start laughing, my hand running along the top of possibly the ugliest kitchen table in the entire world.

"You okay?" Kelsey pockets her phone and walks toward me cautiously.

I shake my head, smiling. "Why would anyone ever let me buy such hideous shit?" My laughter takes the sting out of the words.

Kelsey smiles. "Do you really need to ask?"

"No. I don't."

We have all this ugly shit because Adam loved me enough to let me have everything I wanted.

I love him. I know I do.

I know it through the very depth of my being and I'm on pins and needles just wanting to be with him, to help him, and to tell him.

There's no way this can wait until he's back home in a couple of days.

"Okay then." Kelsey claps her hands together and heads toward the front door. "There's a direct flight in just about four hours. You'll have to wait for a few hours, but it's the best I could do. Zander's going to get a hold of Adam and find out where he's going to be, but he's promised not to tell him why he needs to know."

I follow Kelsey out the door, nodding like I'm listening, but I'm not.

I'm as nervous as a virgin on prom night.

TWENTY-ONE

I don't get into the Des Moines airport until ten o'clock, and by the time I rent a car and drive to the hotel, it's after midnight. I'm exhausted but so hopped up on adrenaline that I feel like I could still run a marathon.

I flip-flop between getting my own room or finding Adam's and confessing everything. Maybe I'll have more control, be calmer, if I sleep on everything for the night and let the memories that have returned settle into something more peaceful.

Right now, I feel like a volcano ready to explode. Everything is bubbling right under the surface of my skin and just waiting to erupt.

But I can't wait.

I've made Adam wait long enough, and now, knowing everything that we went through to be together, I feel like such a bitch in how I've treated him. How amazing he is for sticking by me for the last few months, never leaving my side or completely giving up on me with my insane breakdowns.

I have taken my anger and frustration out on him when he's the one who has kept me grounded.

He's made me brave.

He's made me strong.

And there's nothing I want to do more than be able to do the same thing for him.

With a deep breath, I walk through the lobby of the Heartland Hotel, where I know he's staying, thanks to Zander. I ignore the front desk and head straight for the elevators like I belong there.

My hands fidget nervously along the hem of my shirt and I smooth the wrinkles out of my pants. Except, I'm wearing jeans and they don't wrinkle. I feel like such a wreck.

My heart is doing jumping jacks inside my chest, pounding faster and louder with every step I take down the hallway to his room.

I freeze outside his hotel room, one hand raised to knock on the door. My knuckles rap on the wood three times, then four, before I use both hands to hold the shoulder strap of my overnight bag. My eyes look all over the hall and my feet won't stay still as I fidget back and forth—waiting for him to come to the door.

But he doesn't come.

What if he isn't here?

I raise my hand to knock again, but I stop and dig my cell phone out of my bag. Maybe I should call him first. He's probably sleeping and won't hear me knocking, but he always has his phone next to him.

I step away from his door and dial his number. The phone shakes against my ear as I hold it, but he doesn't pick up. I can hear it ringing inside of his room, but he doesn't answer. I can't believe he'd ignore my phone call.

Slipping my phone into my back pocket, I raise my hand and knock on his door. Louder this time, but he still doesn't answer. Nothing greets me on the other side of the door besides complete silence, and I don't know what to do now.

Where could he possibly be at midnight?

I slink to the floor and rest my head against the wall next to his door. My adrenaline must have crashed because I suddenly feel completely defeated. My head drops back against the wall and I close my eyes, taking deep breaths to calm down and figure out what to do next.

I can always get my own room. I can wait until tomorrow to see him or come back later and see if he's back yet.

My eyes burn with unshed tears and the ring box burns a whole in my pocket as I wonder where he could possibly be on the night before he has to go before a parole board and, for the first time in his life, tell someone the story of what happened the night his mom died.

Suddenly, I know exactly where he will be.

I pick up my bag and toss it over my shoulder. I don't feel nearly as nervous heading to the hotel bar as I did on my way to the room. I know Adam better than anyone now.

He's probably there, elbows resting on the bar, with his hands tearing apart the label on a Sam Adams beer bottle. Something I now know he only does when he's nervous or angry.

I smile in the elevator and it doesn't disappear when I step out of it again, picturing the frown line between his eyes that I imagine he has, thinking about what he has to do and what he has to say.

With a confidence that somehow emerged in the elevator ride, I walk through the lobby and enter the bar with my shoulders straight back and my eyes straight ahead. There are a half-dozen men and women sprinkled through the small and darkened bar, but there is only one man sitting at the bar.

I almost laugh when I see him on the barstool, end of the bar, elbows at the edge, just like I imagined he would be.

I *do* know him.

Slowly, I walk up behind him and take a seat next to him. He doesn't look at me until he hears the thump of my bag hitting the floor.

He glances at the bag, and then at me, before turning away for a split second.

Then his head snaps back to mine. His eyes fly open and his jaw drops to the bar.

"Hi," I say, softly but confidently.

His eyes grow. "What?" He shakes his head as if he can't believe I'm really here. He probably can't believe I'd do this for him. "Are you okay? What are you doing here?"

I take a deep breath.

The speech I've rehearsed over and over for the last six hours is immediately forgotten, and I blurt out, "You let me buy shitty furniture because I always felt like I lived in a museum."

A tear falls down my cheek, but I don't brush it away. I want him to see how much he means to me. He frowns and reaches for me, clearly confused.

"I don't get it."

"I know," I tell him, and hold his hand with mine, resting both on my knee. "I know," I repeat with conviction. "I know that I only went on a first date with you because you won our bet and got an A on your statistics midterm. I know that you let me cry on your shoulder when I told you all about my mom and how I would never be good enough for her. I know you chased me out of your frat house the night Tina jumped into your arms, and we walked around campus for two hours that night because I didn't want to go back to the party, but you didn't want to tell me good night. I know you call me Ames because it's the town where your mom grew up."

I wipe away a tear and continue. "I know that you bought me a camera for Christmas because you knew it was my favorite hobby in the entire world, and you wanted me to bring everything else to light like you told me I did for you . . . brought you out of the darkness. I know that my parents didn't scare you away even when we were kicked out of my parents' house during Thanksgiving dinner."

I take a deep breath. "I know that the only reason I was brave enough to quit the job offered to me at my dad's old firm was because you gave me the strength to be whoever I wanted to be."

"Amy," he says, and leans forward, brushing tears off my cheeks, and one side of his lips lifts into a small grin. "What in the hell are you doing here?"

I laugh through my tears. "Because I went for a walk to the cliffs with Kelsey this morning."

His eyes widen. "The cliffs?"

I nod and close my eyes. "I remembered. The mudslide. Everything."

I reach into my pocket and pull out the light blue box. He looks at my hand and the longest and loudest breath escapes his lips. I place it on the bar and slide it toward him, but he doesn't touch it.

"I haven't opened it. I found it in the box in our closet with all of our pictures. I remember everything, Adam. I don't know how it happened, but everything just flooded my mind today, and as soon as it happened, I knew I had to come here. To be with you."

His lips are on mine, hard and fast, before I can blink. He doesn't deepen it. He just pulls me to him, pressing me against his lips, his hand holding my neck firmly.

He pulls away, taking a deep breath, but I hold him close. My lips just brush his.

"I love you, Adam," I whisper to him softly.

His fingers dig into my skin and his eyes close tightly. When he opens them, his own eyes are wet and filled with unshed tears.

"I was starting to think I'd never hear you say that again."

"I know," I choke out. I'm completely losing control of myself. "But I do. Now that I know everything, can see everything so clearly . . . I'm so sorry for doubting you. Doubting us."

"Don't," he scolds me, and he looks serious. His eyes glance at the ring box on the bar and back to me. "Don't be sorry. Maybe I should have told you from the beginning. I just didn't know the right thing to do." His hand on my neck loosens and slowly runs down my arm to the bar, and then he is holding the box in his hands.

My heart skips a beat and I smile nervously.

"So you didn't look at it?" I shake my head, and his eyebrows pull together. "Do you not want—"

"Oh, I want," I say, cutting him off. I chew on my bottom lip, staring at the box. "I just thought you should be the one to give it to me."

His tongue runs slowly across the top of his lip. Slowly and seductively.

I have the sudden urge to grab him by the neck and kiss him until our lips are swollen. But we're in public, so I refrain. Barely.

"I see," he says, and holds the box.

He stares at it but doesn't open it, and I frown, wondering why he isn't giving it back to me, asking me to marry him—again.

He slips it into his pocket as he climbs off the barstool. Then he puts a twenty-dollar bill on the counter, nodding at the bartender. He reaches for my hand with one hand and grabs the strap of my bag with the other.

I let him lift me off the barstool, but my eyes are still on the box in his pocket, now tucked safely and neatly away.

"Do you not want—"

"Oh," Adam says in a voice that makes my insides turn liquid. "I want."

He presses a kiss against my hand in his and smiles at me over it. His eyes are darkened, pupils almost blacking out the amber brown I normally see.

"This just isn't the time or the place."

"Oh." I'm disappointed. But only until Adam pulls me flush against his chest as we reach the elevator bank. The tension between us explodes into a ball of sexual heat.

"Soon, Amy. It will be soon. But I've been waiting for months for you to look at me like this. Seeing me without any doubt or fear or nerves, and right now all I want to do is take you back up to the room and make love to you for as long as I can."

He raises an eyebrow like he's asking for permission.

"Okay," I squeak out in a small voice right as the elevator doors open.

~

We fall onto the bed as soon as Adam drops my duffel bag and lets the door slam shut behind him. Our bodies are tangled together, legs and arms and hands moving in a rush to shed our clothing as soon as possible.

"God, I love you," Adam says huskily as he rips my jeans off my legs and throws them. They land draped over the television and I snort.

"Nice."

"It will be. I promise."

His scruff tickles my chest, and when I laugh, trying to push him away, he takes my hands and pushes them into the mattress next to my head.

His chin brushes across my nipple. The scratchy hair makes me writhe under him.

"Do you like that?" he asks, and brushes his cheek across my other nipple until both my nipples are hardened little buds. I can't decide if I hate the scratchy, ticklish feeling, or if it's the most erotic thing ever.

Adam is smiling at me, knowing exactly how insane he's making me.

"I want you," I tell him as his lips brush against mine.

My hips move against him, feeling his hardness, and I moan, frustrated, when he pulls away from me.

"You do?" He smiles wickedly and presses his erection against me, sliding it up and down, knowing exactly where to press against me.

"Yes."

My back arches and I fight to get my hands free from him, but Adam holds me tighter, moving against me. So close to where I want him, but not nearly close enough.

"Please?" I open my eyes to stare directly at him. "Please, Adam. I love you."

His breath catches and his lips press against mine. "I love it when you beg."

I smirk. "I know."

He smiles and one of his hands loosens its hold on mine and he guides himself into me.

Stretching me. Filling me. Loving me.

He feels absolutely perfect. Made for me.

I sigh into his mouth and press against him. We begin to move slowly, whispering words of affection. I take them all from Adam like precious little candies and I tuck them into my heart, hoping to never forget how he feels ever again.

Hoping I never forget how *I* feel ever again.

We peak together and Adam's body crushes into mine as we breathe heavily against one another. His back is covered in a light sheen of sweat as I wrap my arms around him, squeezing him to me.

"I love you," I whisper against his cheek. Now that I know how I feel, I never want him to doubt it again. I can't seem to stop myself from saying it.

Now I know that I've *never* been able to stop myself from saying it.

I can feel Adam's grin against the crook of my neck. "I love you. More than anything." He shifts and presses his forehead against mine, his eyes closed. "I'm so glad you're here. Thank you for coming."

I hold him even tighter, not caring if his weight crushes me. "There's nowhere else I could possibly be. Not now."

I mean it. Every single word.

TWENTY-TWO

So what exactly is going to happen today?" I ask Adam through the bathroom doorway. I'm standing at the vanity, applying my makeup, fresh from a shower that just caused us both to get clean, then messy, and clean all over again.

My legs are still a little bit shaky from it.

He walks to the doorway, dressed in a pair of black jeans and an actual polo shirt with a collar. The baby blue in his shirt makes his eyes shine—that or the fact that we've had sex five times since we entered the hotel room last night.

Whatever the reason, he's the most gorgeous guy I've ever seen, and my pulse speeds up just looking at him leaning against the doorframe.

He smiles knowingly and my cheeks flush. At least now I don't need blush.

"I have to meet with the parole board in the prison. They'll ask me questions about my dad, and if I think he's a threat to the public, and if I'd be willing to help with his probation. Keep an eye on him if he gets out."

I frown in the mirror, my eyes locked on his. "What are you thinking?"

He sighs heavily and runs his hands through his hair, staring off into space.

"I think he's evil. I never got to tell my story before . . . what it was like living with him as a kid. I have to do this. I have to make sure they hear what kind of monster he really is."

My lips purse. I don't know the right thing to say to him to make him feel better, but I can tell by the dark color in his eyes that Adam hates that he has to do this.

I set my mascara down and go to him, wrapping my arms around him. His head instantly drops to my shoulder. I feel him take a deep breath and his arms tighten around me.

"God, I'm glad you're here."

I pull back and kiss his cheek. "I want to be here for you. I don't know what you need . . ."

"You." He kisses me and then brushes his lips against my cheek, moving back to nibble on my earlobe. I squirm in his arms and he laughs. "Just you."

"Well, then you have everything you need." I pull away and walk back to the mirror, finishing my makeup and smiling haughtily.

"That I do," he confirms seriously, and leaves me to get ready.

Today, it feels as if the last three months are a dream. Something that wasn't quite real. I know we'll have to work things out. I most likely will have doctor's visits to make sure my memory coming back means that everything that was wrong—whatever it was—is better now.

But we're not dealing with it today.

Because today we're making sure Adam's dad stays in jail. I shudder at the thought and go to find Adam.

When I walk through the doorway, he's looking down at the ring box, smiling at the ring that I still haven't seen except for in my memory. But I'm dying to rip it out of his hands so I can feel it on my finger.

"Ready?" I ask.

He snaps the box closed and shoves it into his pocket. My eyes follow it.

"Yup."

I hesitate as he walks toward me, still staring at the box.

"You're not going to ask me?" I raise my eyebrows when he gets closer to me.

He shakes his head with a grin.

"Nope." I frown and squish my nose up. He taps the tip of it and laughs. "I will. But not today. Do you really want to remember getting engaged on the same day we go to prison?"

I scoff. "We're just visiting. And besides," I tell him, grabbing my purse as he leads me out the door, "it's not like I don't already remember you asking me."

"And look how well that day turned out," he mutters.

I pull on his hand, stopping him in the hallway so I can see his face.

He looks . . . guilty?

"That wasn't your fault."

He shrugs and squeezes my hand tightly. "If I hadn't insisted we go there that day, if I had picked somewhere else . . ." His voice trails off. I can only imagine the horror Adam lived through that day.

"Enough. It was an accident, and I don't want to talk about it anymore." I smile and pull him into the elevator, tugging him until his body is flush against mine. "Let's go send your dad to jail."

We laugh at the absurdity. He silences me when his lips find mine, and then we make out like teenagers until the door opens in the lobby. We ignore the judgmental looks on our exit from the wrinkly women with curly blue hair.

~

Walking into a prison is a lot less intimidating than I thought it was going to be. We sign in and are assigned our visitor stickers. We have to leave my purse and empty our pockets into what looks like a small gym locker. Then we're ushered through a metal detector and down a maze of white hallways. I don't know if I was expecting armed guards at every entrance and men in orange jumpsuits raiding the hallways like zombies, but the overall experience is a bit of a letdown.

I'm let down by not being mauled by prison inmates. I shake my head at the ridiculous thought and let out a garbled sound.

"Are you okay?" Adam asks as we're ushered into a waiting room. It's as pleasant as my dentist's office.

"Yup."

I regain control of myself and turn to Adam, who stands with the guard. I'm not allowed into the private meeting room where he'll be meeting with eight members of the parole board. This is my home for the next who knows how long. I have no idea if it'll take hours, or minutes, and I'm suddenly annoyed and flustered that I don't at least have my phone with me.

Although I doubt they have free Wi-Fi in prison.

Adam leans in and kisses my cheek. He squeezes my hand. I wonder if he knows how often he's squeezing it, or if he's just nervous.

"I'll be back soon, okay?"

I nod, not knowing what to say.

"Have I mentioned that I'm really glad you're here with me for this?"

I chew on my bottom lip and nod again, smiling.

"Once or twice. I love you."

He reaches out and cups my cheeks, framing my face in his slightly rough hands. I ignore the security guard watching us.

"When we're done here, we're going to put all of this and the last three months behind us."

"And then?" I choke out.

"Then we get to the good stuff."

He winks and plants a kiss on my lips that still has my head swimming long after he has left the room.

While they're gone, I mindlessly flip through an entire year's worth of *People* magazines. I couldn't care less about the celebrities; I just have nothing else to do with myself. So it's either mindless magazines or my fingernails are going to be a mangled, nasty-looking mess by the time Adam gets back if it takes too much longer.

Just as I'm considering flipping through a ratty-looking motorcycle magazine, the door opens.

My eyes fly to Adam and I'm instantly on my feet and holding him in my arms. His hair is a wreck, like he's been pulling on it for the last hour, and his eyes are red rimmed.

"Are you okay?" I ask, trying to pull away so I can see his face.

Adam feels like he could collapse in my arms. He holds me tightly to him and shakes his head. "That fucking sucked."

I squeeze my eyes closed, holding him quietly and trying to be there for him.

There's nothing I can say that will make him feel better about talking about the abuse he and his mom suffered with for years. The guard clearing his throat is our cue to leave, so we follow him back out into the barren hallways while Adam keeps an arm wrapped around me, leaning his weight on me.

He's exhausted and I want to do nothing else besides take care of him.

$\sim$

I exhale slowly as soon as we enter our apartment on Friday night. It feels so good to be home after the insanity of the last few days. Nothing like getting two years of your memories back in a span of a few hours, traveling across the country, and visiting a prison to wear a girl out.

I have to laugh or I'll cry from exhaustion.

Adam must feel the same because we've been utterly quiet the entire time back from the airport. Both of us lost in our own thoughts. He's barely said anything about his dad or his meeting with the parole board. All I know is they will be meeting with his dad next week for his actual hearing, but they will take Adam's statement into account.

The man could be free in a week. Or back in jail for the next fifteen years before he becomes eligible for parole again.

"Hey." Adam nudges me and I drop my bag on the kitchen table. "You want something to eat?"

I turn to him and grin. "You're going to cook?"

He scoffs and opens our take-out drawer. Of course not.

"Name your pleasure."

You, I think. By the look I give him, Adam clearly knows what I'm thinking.

"Food, woman. What do you want to eat?"

I raise an eyebrow, and I laugh at his exasperated look. "Fine. Pizza is good. Fast and easy."

"That's what she said," he says, laughing, and he smacks me on the rear with a menu.

I roll my eyes. I'm amazed that after just a few days together, our banter is relaxed and . . . loving. I feel like maybe he should be making me pay penance for the last few months of stress and anger. Or there should be an awkwardness. But there's not. It's relaxing and strange at the same time.

"Do you mind if I go take a bath while we wait for our food?" I ask, but Adam's already on the phone with Martino's, ordering gyro pizza.

He waves me away and I skip off to the bathroom, laughing at how much I love that pizza and how thankful I am of the day he took us there when I wanted to go to all of our favorite places.

He took me to every single one of them. And now I know why they're my favorite. And how special they are to me.

I'm soaking in the tub filled with a relaxing bubble soap when Adam walks in. He changed his clothes into a skintight white T-shirt and a pair of green athletic shorts. I almost swallow a mouthful of bubbles.

"I thought you could use this."

He sets a glass of white wine on the counter and I lay my head against the back of the tub, letting out a low moan.

"God, this is good," I say, swallowing a crisp Riesling and closing my eyes. "This feels like heaven."

I look at the glass when I pull it away and frown into it.

Then I look to Adam. He's bending down on the side of the tub, crouched into a squat, and his arms are crossed on the edge of the tub.

He's smiling at me, amused by my frown. "Do you really think I'm so clichéd that I would put an engagement ring into a wineglass?"

He kisses my nose quickly and squats back down. His eyes try to scan every inch of my completely hidden body in the tub. By his frown, I can't tell which one of us is more disappointed.

"Of course not."

"Good," he says, and then he sets the opened blue box on the ledge right next to me.

I drop the glass of wine into my bathwater.

"Oh shit!" I yell, and I dive my hands under the water to get the glass.

Adam's hands grab my arms and I freeze. I look at him, hearing my pulse beating in my ears.

"Leave the glass in the water and look." He nods toward the box. "The first time I gave this to you, I was so nervous that it wasn't as big as you'd expect." He bites his bottom lip and his noses twitches. "You told me—"

"That I couldn't give a shit about the size of a diamond, just that I get to have your arms around me every day for the rest of my life."

He presses his lips together and his eyes get wet. My own eyes water right along with him. I can't believe I just made Adam get teary eyed. I don't know what has made me more emotional—the engagement or seeing him like this.

He swallows slowly and does some sort of man swipe across his cheeks with the back of his hand.

"I want more than anything to know that's still true."

"It is," I tell him without a doubt in the world.

I lean toward him, as much as I can in the narrow tub, and let him take my hands.

The drowned wineglass is completely forgotten.

He takes the ring from the box and holds it right in front of the ring finger on my left hand.

"Will you marry me? Spend forever with me?"

"Yes," I say, swallowing tears. "Again. Of course I will marry you."

Once he slides the ring on my finger, I reach behind his neck and clasp my fingers together. Adam leans over the edge of the tub as our lips meet, but it's awkward and uncomfortable, so I pull him to me.

The next thing I know, he is in the tub with me, completely dressed, and he has me situated so I'm sitting on his lap. I'm straddling him in our narrow bathtub and the bubbles and water are splashing all over the sides of the tub as our arms move ferociously over each other's skin. My hands lift his shirt off his body, and he pulls away when we have to separate so I can pull it over his head.

He leans back, admiring my body with his hands and his eyes.

"I'm the luckiest man in the world. You chose me, twice. I will never let anything bad happen to you again, Amy."

"I know," I tell him with absolute conviction. "I love you."

Adam wouldn't have ever let anything bad happen to me in the first place. The mudslide was an accident and not his fault at all. I only hope someday—and someday soon—he can let go of the guilt he carries.

Our mouths reconnect passionately and we move against one another. My hands free Adam from his gym shorts and he goes to work, pleasing me until the water gets cold and the pizza arrives.

It's the best memory I have of us. Ever.

And I hope I never forget it.

TWENTY-THREE

Seven months later

"Hey, wake up, sleepyhead."

I shift back into Adam's arms, ignoring the sunlight coming in through the windows in our room.

It's freezing cold in Denver right now, and I know we had at least another six inches of snow last night. The only place I want to be today is in his arms, under our warm comforter, with maybe some coffee and sex.

Okay. Lots of sex.

"I don't wanna go," I whine, and laugh when I end up on my back.

Adam's smile is a few inches from me. His elbows are next to my shoulders, propping him up. My eyes roll back into my head when he presses his erection against me and my legs widen instinctively.

"It's Tilly's birthday today," he reminds me.

As if I need reminding. You would think she's turning thirteen with the insane way my mom has been the last few months planning her birthday party.

"Come on, there'll be ponies to ride and everything."

He's joking. But there probably would be ponies if it wasn't the middle of February.

I grin, clasp my hands together behind his neck, tug on his hair, and pull him to me. He lets me, even as he lets out a low laugh that makes my stomach warm.

"I'll come," I tell him right before I crush his lips to mine. "I promise."

He sets out to immediately prove me right. An hour later, we're finally finished with our showers, dressed, and almost ready to head to my parents' house.

"You nervous about today?" he asks, giving me a strange look.

"No, I just know it'll be a lot of planning talk."

Because not only has my mom been insane about Tilly's birthday, but I decided to try to help mend my relationship with her by giving her full reign of planning my wedding.

Adam and I would have preferred to get married last fall in the middle of a park somewhere with our closest family and friends.

Instead, we're getting married in June on the anniversary of my accident and first engagement. And instead of there being our closest friends and family joining us, the guest list—last I heard anyway—is around three hundred of my closest strangers, family, and family friends. I'll know about ten of them.

But it's made my mom happy, and secretly, I enjoyed getting hauled to dress shop after dress shop, trying on thousands of princess-looking dresses.

"What's she on now?" he asks as he struggles with his tie.

This was another concession Adam and I decided on together. My parents are finally starting to accept that I'm not the daughter they wanted me to be, but instead of immaturely shoving it in their faces just to prove my point, we dress how they would like us to whenever we're together.

And on the flip side, the last time we were there, my parents actually smiled at me.

My mom hugged me and then Adam. And when I asked them for help in giving me a loan so I could start my own coffee shop, Hooka Two, they handed it over gladly.

My dad's expertise has been beneficial, and for the first time in my life, I'm doing exactly what I want to do. I run my own business, and Adam's internship for a local home builder is going well, too.

The only thing we're not growing out of is our apartment. I've decided I'm completely in love with the tiny little place and don't want to move anywhere else, even if we can afford it.

"Invitations, I think," I tell him, while finishing up my makeup in the bathroom mirror. "And then we still have flowers and place settings and cakes. Who knew a wedding took so much work?"

"No kidding," Adam says, and not for the first time since my mom turned our wedding into Denver's event of the year. "I think Zander and Kelsey definitely had the right idea."

"You're the one who said it would make my mom happy to do this for me."

"I know," he says, coming up to me and spinning me from the mirror so I'm wrapped in his arms. "But maybe I'm just a bit jealous that Zander's already had the wedding night and you and I have another three months to wait."

He places a kiss in the crook of my neck.

I laugh, but I'm just as jealous as he is. We just got back two weeks ago from their Caribbean destination wedding. It was only Zander and Kelsey, her parents, and me and Adam for the entire week. Fabulous doesn't begin to describe how much fun we had. It was almost like our own honeymoon, just months before the wedding.

"If you'd like," I tell him, kissing the skin above his tie and giggling at his freshly shaven jaw. I take a few steps forward, pushing him backward and into our bedroom. "I can give you a preview of exactly what's to come."

We fall into the bed and our smiles disappear. His eyes go as hazy as I know mine are. I wiggle against him and he moans.

"You're killing me."

"Well, we wouldn't want that."

I hop off the bed before he can stop me and reach down to pick up a new pair of brown leather riding boots on my way out of the bedroom.

"Tease!"

I shut the door to our room on him, laughing. I can't believe this is my life.

≈

"Happy birthday, dear Tilly, happy birthday to you!"

My entire family stands around Tilly's high chair, with her very own personal cake in front of her, laughing while we encourage her to blow out the candles.

"No!" Ann shouts, and grabs the one lit candle right before Tilly's hand grabs it. We watch as she plants her hand directly into the middle of her cake and proceeds to smear it all over her face, getting very little in her actual mouth.

But she loves it.

Tilly's full of giggles as she reaches for another handful and uses both hands to try to lift her cake directly into her mouth. The cake falls apart, but she manages to get one large bit into her mouth. The rest of the icing covers her nose and her cheeks down to her chin. I'm pretty sure she has some in her eyelashes, too.

"Hey, Tilly," I cheer, getting the chubby-cheeked one-year-old's attention. "Where's your head?"

"No!" my mom gasps, and my sister throws her head back, laughing. It takes a quick second for Tilly to register my question. And then she plants her frosting-covered hands directly onto the top of her head.

With happy tears in her eyes, Ann looks at me. She's trying to be mad, but we both know she's not.

"I will get even with you someday for this. When you have your own, you better watch out."

"You'll be old and gray by the time I have a child," I tell her, mocking how much older she is than me. "Wait," I say, reaching for her hair. "Is that one I see there, now?"

She swats my hand away and gives me a playful evil eye.

Adam's warm hand on my hip nudges me closer to him. "I don't know, I think we should try soon."

My eyes widen and I look at him, shocked. We haven't discussed kids at all. Ever.

"You're crazy," I whisper in his ear so no one in my family can hear us.

If my mom knew I was thinking about having kids now, she'd start planning a baby shower.

"Look at her," he says, nodding toward Tilly, who is laughing and getting cleaned up by my sister. "They're fun."

"Yeah, until you're awake all night, changing poopy diapers, and never finding time to shower. And let's not start with the stretch marks." I shudder, but secretly I'm thrilled to know he wants kids. I was never sure with the family he was raised in, and I don't want to pressure Adam to do anything just for me.

He knocks his hip against mine. "We'll have them. And I want them young enough so we have the energy to chase the shit out of them."

"Them?"

"Two. At least."

I smile with tears in my eyes and stand on my tiptoes, leaning in to kiss him. "I love you, you know."

"I know," he says, leaning in and rubbing his cheek against mine. I don't know why he does it, but I love it when he does. "I love you, too. Now go talk to your mom because she has that binder in her hands."

I groan. "Oh my God. The binder. I'm so sick of looking at that freaking thing."

Adam laughs and pushes me toward her. I go willingly. This is the one thing in my life that has brought me and my mom closer together instead of further apart.

I smile and grab a glass of wine and head to our parlor, where I know my mom already has the binder spread out on the coffee table, waiting for me.

"Hi," I say, sitting down next to her.

I don't think our relationship will ever be close or easy.

But ever since I gained back my memory, I can look back and see the mistakes I made as well as the ones she did. In my hurry to have my own life, I was pretty disrespectful. My parents have never wanted anything but the best for me. Just because I didn't agree with them on how they wanted me to achieve that didn't mean I needed to throw my changing life in their face either.

It hurt her. It hurt both of them, but my mom took it more personally.

So over the last several months, I've tried being honest with my mom with what I'm feeling, as well as being my own person.

"Here's what I'm thinking for invitations," she says, and lays out a spread of at least a dozen of them in front of me.

They're elegant and beautiful. I couldn't care less about invitations for my wedding as long as people show up.

Inwardly, I roll my eyes. Outwardly, I smile and settle in next to my mom.

We spend hours going over flowers and invitation designs that must match the programs and nameplates on the tables. The whole time, I sip my drink, refilling it once or twice, and smile.

In the end, she's happy.

And I get to spend the rest of forever with Adam.

And really, that's all that matters to me.

ACKNOWLEDGMENTS

Writing is such a solitary activity, where I live inside my own head for days, not speaking to anyone, with a dazed look in my eyes. I am so thankful to have the love and backing of my family and closest friends, who support me and occasionally drag me out of my fictional world to join the land of the living.

Thank you, most of all, to my husband. You support and encourage me at every opportunity. You are my greatest cheerleader, my favorite brainstormer, and my best friend. And to my children, I love you to the moon and back. Thank you for understanding that sometimes Mommy needs to write. I hope you don't get upset with all the extra video games I force you to play while I'm under deadline.

To Natalie Gerber and Amanda Halvorson and Rachel Wilson. Thank you for diving into my books, for loving them as much as I do, and for making them better. I treasure all of you!

To Samien, thank you for being you. You make me smile and laugh, and I love being able to talk books with you.

A huge thank you to my Badass CP's: Brittainy, Claire, Amy, Tonya, Kelsie, and Abbie. I'm honored to know all of you. Thank you for your encouragement and help. I'm so thankful to be connected to such a supportive group of writers where we can celebrate each other's accomplishments.

To Taylor, my editor. I promise, you that, someday I will learn, how to use commas, appropriately. Thank you for going through this manuscript with a fine-tooth comb and making it better than anything I could have imagined.

To *Love Between the Sheets* book blog. I LOVE YOU! Thank you for organizing the cover reveal and blog tour. To all the other bloggers, thank you for the time you take to read, review, and support indie authors! All of us authors depend on you, and I'm so grateful for all the women I've had the privilege of getting to meet and know on this crazy journey.

To you—the reader. Thank you. Thank you, thank you, thank you. You make me smile every day with your messages and e-mails. I still can't believe I wrote a book. I'm still in even larger shock that people read them and like them! You make this crazy hobby of mine possible. You make it enjoyable and crazy and exciting and I wish I could tackle hug every single one of you.

And most importantly, thank you to my Heavenly Father and Savior. Your grace and mercy is new every morning. Your love is larger and greater and deeper than anything I could possibly imagine. Thank You for loving me and blessing me.

POINT OF RETURN

Also by Stacey Lynn
Available Now

~

Deceit. Destruction. Death.

Olivia Masters grew up familiar with all of them. The daughter of the president of the Nordic Lord's Motorcycle Club, she always knew she wanted nothing to do with any of it. Her plans were made to leave the town she grew up in as soon as she and her boyfriend, Daemon Knight, turned eighteen.

But then she was shot. Her mother killed in front of her. Fleeing became her reality.

Forced to return to her hometown of Jasper Bay five years later, events beyond Olivia's control put her directly back into the life she swore she'd never return to.

Her dad wants her back in the family. Daemon wants her in his bed.

Just as Olivia begins to accept her destiny, history finds a way to repeat itself.

This time, will Olivia be strong enough to fight for the family she once turned her back on? Or will she again flee from the only life that has ever felt like home?

ABOUT THE AUTHOR

Stacey Lynn lives in Minnesota with her husband and four young children. She spends her day taking care of the kids and loving her family. At night she's curled up with a book and a blanket, or her laptop, writing down all the stories she hears in her head.

She is the author of Amazon and Barnes and Noble bestseller *Don't Lie to Me*, and Amazon bestseller *Point of Return*, as well as the author of *Just One Song* and *Just One Week*.

For more information about Stacey Lynn and her upcoming books, visit:

Facebook: www.facebook.com/staceylynnbooks
Twitter: @staceylynnbooks
Website: staceylynnbooks.blogspot.com
E-mail: staceylynn.author@gmail.com